The CHICKEN'S CURSE

The CHICKEN'S CURSE

FRANCES WATTS

Illustrations by Kelly Canby

ALLEN&UNWIN

SYDNEY•MELBOURNE•AUCKLAND•LONDON

First published by Allen & Unwin in 2020

Allen & Unwin
83 Alexander Street
Crows Nest NSW 2065
Australia
Phone: (61 2) 8425 0100
Email: info@allenandunwin.com
Web: www.allenandunwin.com

 A catalogue record for this book is available from the National Library of Australia

ISBN 978 1 76052 556 9

For teaching resources, explore
www.allenandunwin.com/resources/for-teachers

Illustration techniques: Blackwing pencil with digital colouring (cover); ink and pencil (internals)

Cover and text design by Mika Tabata
Set in 13/15 pt Adobe Jenson by Midland Typesetters, Australia
Printed in Australia by McPherson's Printing Group

10 9 8 7 6 5 4 3 2 1

 The paper in this book is FSC® certified. FSC® promotes environmentally responsible, socially beneficial and economically viable management of the world's forests.

www.franceswatts.com

To Mom and Mike, with love and cake.

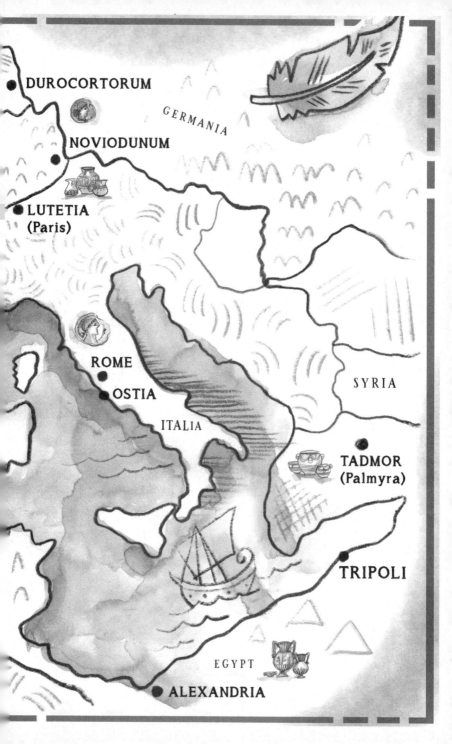

*There once was
a sacred chicken*

*Who thought grain was
no good for lickin'*

*It would only eat cake—
Oh, what a mistake!*

*For too much and the chicken
might sicken.*

Titus Magius

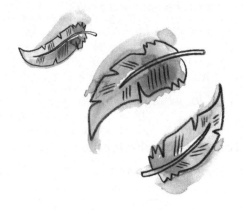

Chapter 1

'Hey, look at that huge serpent over by the general's tent!'

'Wow, I've never seen one that big before. And it's slithering from left to right. Um, isn't that a bad omen?'

'I thought it was bad luck if it slithered from right to left.'

'No, no, that's only when the moon is full.'

Inside the general's tent, Felix glanced up from the helmet he was polishing. A serpent of extraordinary size slithering from left to right *was* a bad omen, he reflected gloomily. Yet another one! Bad omens seemed to follow General Fabius Maximus Porcius around like a bad smell. That very morning, for example, the general's horse had started weeping. The general had said it was nothing, that the horse had allergies, but everyone knew a weeping horse was bad luck.

Felix glanced over at the couch where the general lay to see if he had heard the soldiers talking. Judging by his gentle snores, he hadn't. Though even if he had, it probably wouldn't have changed his mind about going into battle tomorrow against the Nervians who were gathered on the other side of the river. The general was as stubborn as he was unlucky. He had been ignoring all the bad omens, and all the bad signs and portents and auspices too – which was bad news for Felix. For if the general lost the battle, the Nervians would overrun their camp and Felix would be taken prisoner. He'd probably be made a slave and have to spend the rest of his life here in Gallia Belgica, the most cold and rainy corner of Gaul. His heart sank at the thought that he might never see Rome again.

As if to mirror his dark thoughts, a dark shadow appeared behind him in the polished surface of the helmet. Fearing some other sign of ill fortune, Felix turned his head cautiously. Behind him was a tall, thin broomstick of a man wearing a loosely draped toga and a tight frown. It was the augur, who interpreted the will of the gods. And though his expression was grave, Felix felt a spurt of hope. The weeping horse might not have convinced the general to call off the battle, but surely the augur could.

The augur waved his crooked wand at the general's couch. 'Wake him,' he ordered.

'Yes, sir.' Felix stood up and approached the slumbering Porcius. 'General?'

'Hmph?' The general rolled over. He opened his eyes and gazed at Felix blearily. 'What is it?'

'The augur is here, sir.'

The general heaved a sigh. 'Is he, by Jupiter? I suppose I'd better hear what he has to say.'

The augur stepped forwards. 'Sir,' he intoned in a hollow voice, 'I have been reading the skies.'

Felix didn't see how that was possible – you couldn't even see the sky. In the months since they had been sent to this soggy corner of Gaul, the clouds had barely lifted. Or if they had, it was impossible to tell because of the fog. Felix thought longingly of Rome's blue skies and warm air.

'Well?' prompted the general.

'The signs are bad. Very bad. It would be a big mistake to go into battle tomorrow.'

'You're sure you didn't misread the signs? Perhaps you thought you saw a crow but it was actually a dove.'

'I believe I can tell the difference between a crow and a dove, sir,' the augur said icily. 'The gods have been very clear: if you fight the Nervians tomorrow, you will suffer a terrible defeat.'

'Maybe you were looking in the wrong direction,' said the general. 'Or you got your left and right mixed up. Maybe I should come and see the skies for myself, just to be sure.'

'Very well, sir.' The augur pursed his lips.

The general stood up and strode towards the tent's opening. Almost immediately, he stumbled over a black cat passing the entrance.

The stumble and the cat were both unlucky, Felix noted glumly.

'It's another bad omen,' said the augur as they stepped outside.

'Forget your omens,' the general said. He gestured to a unit of soldiers practising drills and formations. 'Look at them. The Roman army is the bravest, most disciplined, most well-armed fighting force the world has ever seen, and the Nervians are just some raggle-taggle Belgic tribe. Who cares if there are forty thousand of them and only twenty-five thousand of us?'

Forty thousand Nervians! Felix repressed a gulp. How did the Nervians treat their slaves? he wondered.

The general tilted his head back to gaze at the sky. 'Well?' he said. 'What's the problem? I don't see any—'

Crack!

Felix winced as lightning crashed on the horizon.

'The gods are unhappy,' said the augur.

The general fixed him with a frosty stare. 'You don't say.' He turned on his heel and strode back into the tent.

Felix followed reluctantly and picked up his cloth to resume polishing the general's armour. It seemed nothing could stop the battle from going ahead now. If only the Nervians weren't so famously fierce ...

There was a discreet cough behind him.

It was the augur again, and with him was a man wearing a tunic covered in feathers.

'Excuse me, General,' said the augur.

'You again?' said General Porcius. 'What is it this time? Did you hear the hoot of a murderous owl?'

'No, sir,' said the augur.

'Has a magpie approached you from behind?'

The augur shook his head. 'No, it's not that.'

'Have you seen a serpent of extraordinary size slithering from left to right?'

Felix opened his mouth then closed it again.

'No,' said the augur.

'Then what is it?' the general demanded.

'It's the chickens.'

The general frowned. 'What chickens?'

The man in feathers replied, 'The sacred chickens.'

The chickens – of course! All those other bad omens counted for nothing if the sacred chickens were in favour of the battle.

The general squinted at the feathered man and said, 'You're the one who looks after them, aren't you?'

'I am, sir.'

'So you've released them, the sacred chickens?'

'I have, sir.'

'And?'

'They won't eat their grain.'

The general rolled his eyes. 'Of course,' he said. 'Silly sacred chickens.'

Felix kept his eyes on his work, but inside he was elated. There was no way the general would ride into battle if the sacred chickens had refused their grain. History was full of examples of what happened to those who failed to heed such an auspicious warning. Take Publius Claudius Pulcher, who had ordered the sacred chickens to be flung into the sea when they refused to eat. 'If they won't eat,' he had famously declared, 'perhaps they will drink.' The next day he had suffered a mighty defeat against the Carthaginians.

'So, we'll abandon the battle?' the augur said.

The general crossed his arms. 'No, we will not.'

'But the chickens ...'

'May Jupiter strike them dead!'

Felix, the augur and the keeper of the sacred chickens all gasped.

'The chickens are wrong,' the general declared.

Wrong? Felix gaped at the general in disbelief. The chickens were never wrong! Just ask Publius Claudius Pulcher.

The augur and the chicken keeper left the tent, muttering darkly about the general's foolishness. Yet far from being cowed by the chickens, General Porcius seemed to be filled with a new sense of determination. 'Oi, Rufus!' He snapped his fingers at Felix.

'It's Felix, sir,' Felix told the general for what seemed like the thousandth time.

'Don't tell me what your name is. Roman boys with red hair are always called Rufus. You're Roman. You have red hair. Therefore your name is—'

'Still Felix, sir.'

'Well, whatever your name is, I want you to fetch the centurions. It's time to go over the battle plans. We'll show those chickens what's what.'

The general walked over to the table in the centre of the tent and unrolled a map.

Felix flung down his polishing cloth and set off to follow the general's orders. He'd had it with the army. The general might dismiss the omen of the sacred chickens, but Felix couldn't. There was nothing else for it – he would have to run away. Away from the ferocious Nervians and the unlucky general. Away from the grey skies of Belgica. Back to sunshine, and his mother's cooking. Back to Rome.

Chapter 2

Later that night, Felix lay on the floor at the foot of General Porcius's bed, shivering beneath the thin blanket.

Above him, the general was snoring and snuffling in his sleep.

This was his chance. Felix threw off the blanket, slipped on his sandals and his heavy felt cloak, and began to tiptoe across the tent. He was almost at the opening when the general's snoring abruptly ceased.

Felix froze.

He stood motionless in the dark, heart pounding, until at last the general let out a giant belch then returned to his snoring.

When his legs had unfrozen enough to move, Felix resumed his tiptoeing. Carefully pushing aside the tent's flap, he peered out.

The sentry who was drowsing in the entrance, leaning on his spear, opened an eye.

'Urgent call of nature,' Felix whispered. 'I think the eels we had for dinner must have been off.'

'Mmmph,' said the sentry.

For once the moon was visible in the sky, cold and bright among a scattering of stars. *The goddess Luna must be smiling on me*, Felix thought. After a year in the company of General Porcius, it made a pleasant change to be favoured by the gods.

Trying to seem like someone in a desperate hurry to use the latrines – rather than someone in a desperate hurry to escape a battle that would end in certain defeat – Felix walked quickly through the camp. Past the tent containing the standards, long poles topped with silver eagles and flags representing each legion. Past the horses whickering softly in the stables. Along a row of tents in which the soldiers slept.

Ahead he could see the main gate, which looked north down a grassy slope to the river. On the other side of the river was the enemy. No, thank you, Felix decided. He would use the smaller western gate, from where it was only a short distance into the forest that surrounded the camp on three sides.

He continued moving silently between the rows of tents until he could see the gate, which was overlooked by a watchtower. In it, he knew, were two sentries standing guard. But though he watched for several minutes, there was no movement, no murmuring ... it seemed the sentries must be asleep.

He waited a few more minutes, then, as the moon disappeared behind a cloud, Felix slipped through the gate.

'Who goes there?' The voice rang loudly in the still night.

Oh no!

Felix sprinted across the stony ground, heading for the cover of the forest.

Behind him, he could hear the clatter of footsteps as the sentries descended from the watchtower, spears and armour clanking.

'There!' said one. 'I think I see him!'

'Quick!' said the other. 'Don't let him get away!'

Felix ran for his life through the dark night, stumbling over the stones he couldn't see, heart thundering in his chest. General Porcius was merciless when it came to deserters; he would probably give Felix to the Nervians himself.

Oak trees loomed large in front of him. He was almost there!

'Get him!' shouted a sentry.

Gasping for breath, his lungs burning, Felix put on a desperate burst of speed.

And then three things happened in quick succession ...

The clouds covering the moon parted again.

Felix dived into a bush.

The bush let out a loud squawk.

Time seemed to freeze. Felix lay panting among the leaves, expecting at any moment to feel the heavy hand of a sentry or the sharp point of a spear.

Instead, he heard one of his pursuers say: 'Did you see that flash of red? We've been chasing a fox this whole time. And you know what that squawk means: he stole himself a chicken for his supper.'

'I wish *I* had a chicken for my supper.'

'We'd better get back before anyone notices we're not at our posts. If we're asked, we were chasing a spy, okay?'

'With mushrooms and leeks.'

'I don't think we need to mention leeks. There wasn't really a spy.'

'Not the spy – the chicken. Why would you want to eat a spy?'

'What?'

As the sentries bickered their way back across the stony ground to the camp, Felix lay still, his heart thudding. When at last their voices had faded, he extracted himself from the leaves – with what seemed like an extraordinary amount of rustling.

Standing upright, he was confronted by a hooded figure.

He screamed.

The hooded figure squawked, then said, 'Quiet!'

It was a girl's voice.

Felix stared at her in surprise.

She was wrapped in a cloak that, even in the weak glow of the moon penetrating the forest's canopy, he could tell was made of fine wool. Certainly it was finer than his rough garment. She pushed the hood back to reveal long, dark hair and a long, straight nose down which she was staring at Felix – a remarkable feat, he thought, given that she was the same height as him.

'Who are you?' he asked.

'What does it look like? I'm a sacred chicken.'

He was so astonished by this declaration that he just goggled at her in amazement for several seconds.

'You're a chicken?' he said finally. Obviously the girl was not in her right mind. She was clearly the daughter of a senator or a provincial governor or a consul – not the daughter of a rooster and a hen.

'Not her, you fool – me. Down here.'

Felix looked down to see a rather annoyed chicken.

He looked up to see a rather annoyed girl.

'You thought I was a chicken?' she said.

'I didn't know chickens could talk,' he protested.

'I'm a *sacred* chicken,' the chicken said emphatically, as if that explained it.

'So who are *you?*' he asked the girl.

'I can't see how that is any of your business,' she replied in a voice as haughty as her stare.

Felix shrugged. 'All right then. Well, I'll be off.'

'Wait!' said the girl. 'Where do you think you're going?'

'Rome.'

'Why?' she demanded.

Felix considered saying, *I can't see how that is any of your business*, but realised that she might decide it was the business of the sentries. Floundering for a reason why he might be skulking in the forest in the dead of night, he said, 'I'm … I'm carrying an urgent message for General Fabius Maximus Porcius.'

'You're a messenger,' she said. There was a note of disbelief in her voice.

'That's right,' Felix replied.

'Where's the message?'

She was looking him up and down, and Felix cursed himself for not having come up with a better excuse.

'Don't messengers carry scrolls?'

'It's a very secret and important message,' Felix improvised. 'So secret and important the general didn't want to write it down.'

'Then how can you deliver it?'

'I've memorised it.'

'Is that right,' said the girl. It didn't sound like a question.

There was a moment's silence, then she barked: 'What did you have for dinner two nights ago?'

'T-two nights ago?' Felix stammered. 'I-I don't know. I can't remember.'

'I knew it.' The girl sounded smug. 'No one would trust you to memorise a secret message. I bet you can't even remember your own name.'

'Of course I can,' said Felix, stung. 'It's Felix.'

'And you're not really a messenger, are you, Felix?'

'No,' he confessed with a sigh. 'I'm running away.'

'I never would have guessed,' said the girl, though it was apparent she had.

'I'm General Porcius's servant. I'm on my way home to Rome so that I don't get turned into a slave by the Nervians. Tomorrow's battle has been cursed.' Felix pointed at the chicken. 'By you.'

The girl turned her gaze to the chicken. 'What's your story?' she asked.

'I told you: I'm a sacred chicken,' the chicken said. It sounded as haughty as the girl.

'Why did you curse the battle?'

'I don't know about the others, but I just didn't feel like grain.' The chicken tossed its head so that its wattles shook. 'I can't help it if I'm a picky eater.'

'So what are you doing here?'

'I'm running away too. I'm going to Rome, where the sacred chickens are fed on cake. I like cake.'

'You're going all the way to Rome on your own?'

'Why not?' said the chicken.

'Aren't you scared of foxes?'

'No,' said the chicken defiantly, but Felix thought he detected a tremor in its comb.

'You'll never make it to Rome on your own either,' the girl said to Felix. 'Think about it: wolves, bandits, Nervians. And what about when the general finds out you're gone? He'll probably send someone after you.'

Felix knew the girl was right. He'd been foolish and impulsive. There was no way he was going to get away with this. He should go back to camp. Perhaps if he told the sentries he'd been sleepwalking …

'It's your lucky day,' the girl announced.

That seemed unlikely, thought Felix.

'I'm going to Rome, too. The general's men will be looking for a boy travelling alone, so I'll let you travel with me.'

'What about me?' said the chicken. 'You can't leave me here.'

'Why not?' said the girl.

'I'm a sacred chicken. If you abandon me to the foxes, you'll be cursed.'

The girl looked at Felix.

'The chicken's right,' Felix said. 'We can't leave it.'

The girl sighed. 'Fine. We'll all go.'

They began to wind their way between the trees in single file, following what might have been a path, or a track used by animals, or just the random whim of the girl, who was in the lead.

'So why are you travelling alone?' Felix asked her. Someone of noble birth should be safe in a carriage, attended by servants or slaves, not wandering through the forest in the middle of the night.

'I'm not travelling alone,' she replied. 'I'm travelling with you and the chicken.' Felix could tell by her voice that she was rolling her eyes.

They walked in silence for a while, Felix glancing over his shoulder every now and then to check if they were being followed. A faint lightening of the sky above the forest's canopy suggested the approach of dawn. It was only a matter of time before General Porcius noticed he was missing.

As the first tendrils of sunlight crept between the leaves, the track they'd been following met up with a path.

The girl hesitated, looking from left to right. 'Which way, do you think?' she asked, turning to Felix.

The light was coming from behind them, so they must be facing west, Felix reasoned. That meant left was south and right was north. Rome, he knew, was south.

'Left,' he said. And then, recalling the route the army had taken all those wet, soggy months ago, he said, 'We should reach a road to Durocortorum.'

'Is that a kind of cake?' asked the chicken.

'No.'

'I know Durocortorum,' the girl said. 'It's a big town. We can try to get seats in a fast carriage heading in the direction of Rome. That will be far quicker than walking.'

The path was wider than the track had been, and Felix and the girl were able to walk side by side. Now they'd be able to talk properly.

'The sooner we get to Rome the better,' Felix began. 'My mother will be pleased to see me. She'll probably tell me I shouldn't have deserted, but I'm sure she'll understand when I explain it. And I've got two sisters – they'll be pleased to see me too.' Actually, he wasn't so sure of this. His sisters sometimes talked to him as if he were a fool and at other times refused to talk to him at all. They were a lot like this girl, in fact.

'Do you have a brother?' he asked her.

She didn't respond.

'Do you live in Rome?'

Nothing.

'Do you have a name?' he asked.

The girl hesitated, as if reluctant to reveal confidential information.

'Livia,' she said finally.

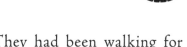

They had been walking for several hours, up and down what seemed like an endless series of hills, when the path emerged from the forest. Felix blinked. It had been hard to tell what time it was in the forest, as only a meagre amount of light had penetrated the thick canopy, but now he saw that the sun was quite high in the sky. At least, Felix presumed it was the sun. Something was glowing beneath the cover of grey.

Looking behind them, Felix saw the road curving out of sight behind a hill. The section before them was long and flat, the flagstones glinting here and there where water had pooled in the crevices. On either side were fields, separated from the road by ditches.

While the trees had felt oppressive, a haven for bandits, now that they'd left the forest behind he felt exposed. They'd have nowhere to hide if they were pursued.

The chicken didn't seem at all concerned to be out in the open.

'I'm hungry,' it complained. 'What have you got to eat?'

'Didn't you bring anything with you?' Livia asked.

'In what? My basket?' The chicken stared pointedly at the basket Livia was carrying. 'I presume you have some food in there.'

'Why should I share it with you?'

'Oh, you don't have to,' said the chicken. 'Though denying food to a sacred chicken isn't going to bring you good fortune for your journey, is it?'

'He's right,' said Felix.

Livia sighed. 'I suppose I could give you some bread.'

'That'll have to do,' the chicken grumbled.

'Listen!' Felix broke in. 'I think I hear something behind us.'

They all turned around.

No one was visible, but the clatter of hooves on stone was unmistakable.

'Into the ditch!' Livia ordered. 'Quick!'

'My feathers will get wet!' the chicken protested.

As he dived into the ditch, Felix scooped up the sacred chicken in one arm.

They crouched in the muddy trench as the hooves drew closer and closer. Had the riders seen them? Felix felt water seeping through his clothes, yet he didn't dare move.

As the thunder of hooves sounded right above their heads, he heard snatches of conversation.

'—ran off last night—' a voice boomed.

'—can't have got very far on foot—' came a shrill reply.

They were talking about him!

His body tensed, causing him to squeeze the chicken, which pecked his armpit viciously.

Suppressing a yelp, he relaxed his grip. The chicken promptly wriggled free.

Squawk!

'Shhhh!' Felix and Livia hissed in unison.

Squawk!

Felix held his breath, praying to Jupiter that the men hadn't heard. But the hooves thundered by, and gradually faded.

When his heart had ceased thundering too, Felix burst out: 'Did you hear what those men said? They were looking for me!'

'No,' the chicken corrected him. 'They were looking for *me*.'

Livia said nothing, though as they clambered from the ditch, she appeared strangely subdued. Her brow was furrowed and she gnawed her bottom lip while staring down the road after the riders.

As he wrung out his cloak Felix was struck by a thought. 'You didn't need to jump in the ditch, Livia. The men weren't after you.'

Livia turned her gaze away from the road to look at him. 'I decided it would be safer to hide. What if they asked me if I'd seen you and I accidentally gave you away?'

Watching as she brushed the mud from her fine cloak, Felix felt touched by her concern. Despite her aloof manner, she cared about what happened to him.

Yet while she had done her best to protect him, the chicken hadn't, he recalled. He frowned at the chicken. 'Why did you squawk like that?' he demanded. 'They might have heard you.'

The sacred chicken shrugged. 'I can't help it. I'm a chicken. Squawking's what we do.'

They carried on down the road, but more cautiously now. Every flicker of a shadow seemed like a warning, and the sound of a pebble clattering across the flagstones like approaching hooves.

The chicken strutted along ahead of them, the plume of its tail feathers held aloft proudly, red comb rippling in the breeze. It was clearly feeling none of their anxiety. Livia whispered to Felix, 'I think we should dump the chicken. It's going to get us caught.'

'We can't dump it,' Felix whispered back. 'We'd be cursed.'

'But it's run away,' Livia argued. 'So it's actually a bad sacred chicken.'

'I heard that!' the chicken yelled.

'She didn't mean it,' Felix said quickly.

'Yes I did,' snapped Livia.

As he tried to soothe the chicken on one hand and appease Livia on the other, Felix felt a wave of weariness wash over him. They'd been travelling together for only a few hours and he was already worn out from trying to keep the peace between the noble girl and the sacred chicken.

Not to mention trying to evade the men who were pursuing him ...

Chapter 3

'We need to get off this road,' Felix said, glancing over his shoulder for what felt like the hundredth time. It had been raining on and off for hours and their cloaks and feathers were sodden, but Felix was so preoccupied by his fear of patrols and pursuers he hardly noticed.

'We have to get to Durocortorum,' Livia reminded him. 'And this is the road that will take us there.'

When, towards the end of the afternoon, they met a traveller coming in the opposite direction, Felix hailed him. 'Excuse me,' Felix said, 'do you know of another way to Durocortorum? We're taking our chicken to market and, um, the hard flagstones are giving it sore feet.'

The man didn't even blink at this wild invention. 'No wonder,' he said, observing the muddy, dishevelled chicken. 'It's so scrawny. Hardly worth putting in a pot. Good luck trying to sell that!'

When the chicken looked like it was about to protest, Livia flung her cloak over it. 'Oops,' she said. 'I dropped my cloak.'

'Just past the next milestone there's a shortcut through the forest to Durocortorum,' the traveller told them. 'Look for the blasted oak on your right – there's a path beside it.'

When the man set off down the road, Livia retrieved her cloak.

The sacred chicken shook itself angrily in a flurry of wet feathers.

'Sell me at the market? As if I was some kind of common barnyard animal? I'll have you know I lived in the finest coop in the legion. The wire was all spun from gold and I had a drinking trough made from marble.'

Felix suspected the chicken must be exaggerating. He'd never seen anything like that around the camp.

'You have never seen such splendour in your life,' the chicken finished.

Livia was unimpressed. 'I'll have you know I happened to live in a very grand—' She stopped abruptly.

'What?' said Felix. 'A very grand what?'

'Nothing.'

He knew it! She was probably from one of Rome's finest families, with a large house on the Esquiline Hill. While Felix, his mother and sisters were crammed into a single room on the fourth floor of a crowded apartment building in Subura, Livia no doubt had a huge atrium and a dining room decorated with mosaics, and slaves serving her honeyed figs while she reclined on a couch in the garden.

'A grand house? A grand villa? A grand mansion?' Felix pressed.

In response, Livia took a large handkerchief from her basket and blew her nose loudly.

'I suppose you bathe in rosewater and scent the soles of your feet with jasmine perfume.'

Shaking her head, Livia tucked the handkerchief back into her basket.

'I suppose you dine on roast peacock every night.'

'Don't be ridiculous,' said Livia, though her lips twitched.

'I suppose you ride to banquets on an elephant,' Felix continued.

'Hmph,' she said, as if he was being too silly for words, but he thought he caught a fleeting smile and, despite the heavy grey clouds pressing down on them, his heart immediately felt lighter.

The lightening of mood was soon dampened by the drizzle.

'This is outrageous,' the sacred chicken declared. 'My comb is waterlogged. The gods will not smile on you for subjecting a sacred chicken to such torment.'

'You should have stayed in your golden coop then, shouldn't you?' Livia retorted.

'What's that in the sky?' Felix jumped in to stop another round of bickering.

Luckily, his ploy worked, as both Livia and the chicken looked up.

And to Felix's relief there *was* something to see in the sky.

'It looks like a bird of prey,' said Livia.

'I think it's an eagle,' said Felix.

'It's probably a chicken,' said the sacred chicken. 'It can be hard to tell chickens and eagles apart when they're in flight.'

Felix couldn't help it; he began to laugh.

'What?' said the chicken crossly as Livia gave Felix a quizzical look.

'Imagine the standard bearers,' Felix said to Livia.

He marched ahead of her along the path holding an imaginary pole. 'See the mighty Roman legions marching into battle with their silver chickens aloft.'

Livia giggled.

'Marching under the symbol of the majestic chicken of Rome!'

Livia giggled some more.

Felix pointed. 'Up there! In the sky! It's a vicious chicken about to attack!'

By now Livia was laughing so hard she'd had to stop walking.

The sacred chicken looked most put out.

'I'm sorry,' said Felix, ashamed for making fun of it.

'I'm not talking to you,' said the chicken.

Livia had stuffed her cloak into her mouth to muffle her laughter, but her shoulders were shaking.

'Go on, laugh away,' the chicken said bitterly. 'I know you don't care about me at all. *Dump the sacred chicken*, you said. *Leave the sacred chicken to die*, you said.'

'I don't think she said we should leave you to die,' Felix objected.

But the chicken ignored him. 'I'll see if I can find a fox to do the job for you, shall I?' And it stormed off into the forest.

'Wait!' said Felix, alarmed. 'Come back!' He rushed after it.

Muttering to itself, the chicken allowed Felix to usher it back to the path.

'Livia, please.' Felix gave her a stern look. 'I think you owe the sacred chicken an apology.'

Livia looked at the chicken and then back at Felix. 'You seriously believe it can curse us?'

Felix thought of General Porcius. 'Yes,' he said. 'I really do.'

'If it means that much to you …' She turned to the chicken. 'I'm sorry,' she said.

'Your apology is accepted,' the chicken said graciously.

The grey sky had turned a bruised purple by the time they reached the milestone, and it was so dark by the time they saw the blasted oak that they almost missed the turn-off into the forest.

'Perhaps we should stop here for the night,' Felix suggested hesitantly, reluctant to venture into the black forest, and to his relief the others agreed.

Livia surveyed the patch of grass and shrubs between the road and the forest. 'We'll need to find some kind of cover from the drizzle,' she declared.

Felix tramped through the tall, wet grass until he found a shrub that seemed to provide a little more shelter than the others. 'Over here,' he called. 'This one's only a little damp.'

'Why would I want to sleep in that damp shrub when it's perfectly dry here in the hollow of this tree?' the chicken called back.

'You found shelter?' said Felix. 'Why didn't you say something?'

'I thought you must have wanted to sleep in a damp shrub, you were going to so much trouble.'

It was a bit of a tight squeeze by the time they were all settled in the hollow, but at least it was warm, and they were well hidden from the road. For the first time since he'd fled the camp, Felix started to relax.

Felix was woken at dawn by the ear-splitting squawking of the chicken.

'Stop it!' he cried.

'I'm a chicken,' the chicken reminded him. 'It's what we do in the morning.' It walked over to Livia's basket and stuck its beak in. 'How about some bread?'

Grumbling sleepily, Livia brushed it away. 'I don't have any more,' she said.

After an unsatisfying breakfast of wild mushrooms foraged from among the pine needles near a stand of trees, they set off along the path leading into the forest. Dark, shadowy pines mingled with the pale trunks of birch and fresh green beech. It would have been almost lovely, Felix thought, if only the patter of rain on the ferns didn't sound quite so much like the footsteps of a patrol creeping through the undergrowth; if only the whistle of wind through the leaves didn't sound like the whistle of a Roman soldier who'd spotted the general's runaway servant.

Of course, it was hard to hear any of these things over the sound of the chicken's sulky mutterings. For the sacred chicken complained endlessly.

He complained when it rained.

'My feet are wet.'

He complained when the clouds parted briefly and the sun shone.

'My feathers are steaming.'

He complained when it was windy.

'My giblets are rattling.'

And most of all he complained about how hungry he was.

As their stomachs rumbled, they talked about their favourite foods.

Felix thought of the meals his mother had served up back in their cramped apartment in Rome. 'Wheat porridge with mushrooms,' he said. 'Or maybe cabbage soup. Or …' Come to think of it, they never seemed to eat anything but wheat porridge and cabbage soup.

Livia said, 'Dormice drizzled in honey and sprinkled with poppy seeds. And for dessert ... a pear soufflé.'

Dormice drizzled in honey? Felix couldn't even imagine the world she came from. It was astonishing that he should find himself travelling with someone of Livia's rank. 'So, are you the daughter of a senator?' he asked.

'No,' she said, her voice short.

'The daughter of a governor, then?'

'No.'

'The daughter of—'

'Leave it, Felix,' she snapped.

Felix felt hurt. He didn't see why she had to be so secretive.

'What about you?' Felix asked the sacred chicken. 'What's your favourite meal?'

'Cake,' said the chicken firmly.

As they passed through a small hamlet – a scattering of houses with thatched roofs surrounded by vegetable plots – they debated stopping to ask for food.

Felix pointed to a rustic cottage with a thatched roof set below the path in a dip between two hills. A broad, red-faced woman was weeding the garden by the side of the house. 'She looks kind,' he said. 'I'm sure she'll help us.'

They strode down the hill towards her.

'Good morning,' Felix said politely. 'We're very hungry and we wondered if you had some food?'

'Why, yes,' said the woman. 'I do.'

As Felix turned to smile at Livia, the woman reached out and grabbed the sacred chicken around the neck.

'I have this chicken,' she said.

'What? But that's *our* chicken!' Felix exclaimed.

'Not anymore, it's not,' said the woman. 'I found it fair and square. And now I'm going to put it in my pot.'

As she tightened her grip around its neck, the chicken began to gasp and cough.

'Stop your cackling, you old boiler,' the woman said, giving the chicken a shake.

'You can't talk to it like that,' said Felix, aghast. 'And you can't eat it. It's a *sacred* chicken.'

'This? A sacred chicken? What do you take me for – a fool?' With her free hand she cuffed Felix's ear. 'A country bumpkin, is that what you think?' She delivered another mighty whack, which landed on Felix's shoulder.

'Ow!'

'Look,' said Livia impatiently, 'this is our chicken and we want him back.'

'If you want him that badly, I'll sell him to you,' said the woman craftily.

'We don't have any money,' Felix said.

'Oh, really?'

The woman fixed her eyes on Livia. 'What have you got in that basket, girly?'

Livia glared at her. 'Do *not* call me "girly",' she ordered.

'Proud one, aren't you? Well, let me put it this way: I'm putting this chicken in my pot unless you make it worth my while not to.'

'Livia?' Felix pleaded.

Even the chicken gazed at her imploringly.

'Very well,' said Livia.

She raised a corner of the cloth that covered her basket and rummaged inside. After several seconds, she produced a gold ring.

The woman's eyes glinted greedily as she reached for it.

'Just a moment,' said Livia, closing her hand around the jewel. 'We'll be wanting more than the chicken for this. We'll need a loaf of bread and some cheese, too.'

'And cake,' added the chicken.

'You should thank Livia for selling her ring to get you back,' Felix said to the chicken.

They had rounded a corner and were sitting on a large, flat rock by the side of the path, enjoying a hearty breakfast.

'Big deal,' said the chicken, which was pecking at a sticky honey cake. It looked up, its beak covered in crumbs. 'She can afford to give away a ring – that basket is stuffed full of jewels.'

Livia glared at it. 'Have you been sticking your nosy beak into my basket?'

'I was hungry,' the chicken defended itself. 'I thought you might have some cake hidden in there. Speaking of which, this cake is ... bery bood ... but bery shhticky.' It seemed to be having trouble getting its beak open.

'Maybe if you didn't eat so fast,' Felix suggested. He closed his eyes to savour the cheese. It was wonderful to eat a proper meal. Some sun on his face, food in his belly, friends by his side – he hadn't felt this content since leaving Rome.

Then a large hand seized him roughly by the arm and a voice boomed: 'Got you!'

Chapter 4

The man who'd grabbed Felix's arm dragged him to his feet. 'What have you got to say for yourself?'

The man was as big and beefy as a bull in a tunic, and his booming voice was familiar. It must be the men they'd heard when they were in the ditch, Felix realised. The men who were after him! He'd been lost in his happy reverie and hadn't even heard them approach.

'I ... I ...' Felix quavered. If the man hadn't held his arm in such a tight grip Felix would have fallen, he was trembling so violently.

'Eh, girl?'

Felix blinked. *Girl?*

Then the other man spoke. 'Hang on, it isn't her. It's a boy.' This man was as slender as a reed with a high, reedy voice.

The larger man dropped Felix's arm, took a step backwards and examined him. 'Well, it's about the right height.'

'Where's the girl?' the smaller man demanded.

Felix looked around. Livia and her basket had vanished.

'Wh-what girl?' he stammered.

'Who were you talking to just now? We heard you talking.'

'M-my chicken. I was talking to my chicken. I-I'm taking it to market in Durocortorum.' Felix's voice came out as a squeak.

'Just the one?' boomed the large man.

'My family is very poor.'

'That explains why you've got such an ugly, scrawny chicken.'

Mmmmmpppph. The chicken's eyes were nearly popping out of its head as it struggled to open its beak, which was still stuck shut from the honey.

'Enough about the chicken,' the reedy man broke in. 'You seen a girl about this high?' He held his hand up level with the top of Felix's head.

'N-no.'

'Well, if you do, you should seize her,' Beefy advised. 'She's a runaway. The governor of Nemetacum wants her back.' He sat down on the rock and stretched out his legs in front of him. 'And he's promised us a big reward if we find her,' he continued as he helped himself to Felix's bread and cheese.

Taking a seat beside him, Reedy took a knife from his belt and sliced off a piece of the honey cake, seemingly unaware of the chicken's frantically flapped objections.

'We've been up and down that road from Durocortorum to Nemetacum and there's been no sign of her. That's why we decided to try this path. But ...' He shrugged helplessly. 'It's like she's vanished.'

It seemed she was good at vanishing. Felix collapsed onto the rock beside the beefy man. *Wait.* It was *Livia* they were after? Not him? His mind reeled.

When the governor's men had finished all the food, they stood up and brushed the crumbs from their tunics.

'If you see her, don't even think about helping her,' Reedy warned. 'The governor will take it very badly.'

'Good luck selling that chicken,' Beefy added. 'You'll need it.'

They set off down the path as Felix, still stunned by the men's revelations, stayed sitting on the rock, which was now surrounded by the crumbled remains of the meal he had so recently been enjoying.

It was Livia they'd been after all along. It explained why she'd been so quick to jump into that ditch when he'd heard the men's horses. But what would make her run away from her luxurious life in the governor's mansion to sit in muddy ditches and trudge through damp forests? 'And why didn't she tell me the truth?' he asked aloud.

There was a whisper from behind him. 'Are they gone?'

'Livia?!' Felix looked around. He couldn't see anyone.

'Down here. Help me up.'

Peering over the edge of the rock, he could make out Livia crouched in the bushes in a hollow.

He extended his hand and helped to heave her back onto the rock.

'I knew it,' Felix said when she was sitting beside him, panting from the effort of the climb. 'You're the governor's daughter, aren't you?'

She shook her head. Her lips were sealed as tight as if they'd been glued shut by honey cake.

'I told you the truth,' Felix said to Livia. 'I told you I deserted from the army. I can't believe you don't trust me.'

'I do trust you,' said Livia. 'It's just ... it's better for you if you don't know the whole story.'

'The whole story? What story?'

She tightened her lips once more and refused to speak. And seeing that she appeared anxious and frightened and not at all haughty, Felix relented.

'Come on,' he said, standing up. 'Durocortorum can't be far.'

As they drew closer to Durocortorum, they made plans. They would need to leave the town as soon as possible now that they knew Beefy and Reedy were patrolling the road. Livia would exchange some of the jewels in her basket for their passage in a carriage.

By the time the path through the forest rejoined the road, they were only a couple of miles from their destination. As they were near the town, there were more people on the road: some on foot and carrying baskets, bound for the market; others driving carts piled high with produce. Livia wore the hood of her cloak over her head so that her face was in shadow.

Finally, they reached a bridge over a river. On the far side was the entrance to the town, guards standing by the gate.

'We made it!' said Felix as he stepped onto the bridge. He felt jubilant. Once they were in the carriage, none of them would have to worry about being pursued anymore. They'd be free!

'This is Rome?' said the chicken, looking around. 'I thought it would be much more impressive.'

'It's not Rome. It's Durocortorum.' *Honestly*, Felix thought, *doesn't the chicken ever listen?* He turned to exchange a look with Livia, but she was no longer beside him.

She had stopped walking and had tilted her head back to watch a crow swooping past her left side from the top of the town walls. The hood of her cloak had slid down to her shoulders.

'Livia,' he called, 'come on.' Surely she knew that to see a crow on your left side was a bad omen. Suddenly, he had an uneasy feeling. 'Livia!' he called again.

Just as she twisted in the direction of his voice, a second voice rose behind them, high and thin. 'There she is!'

Felix spun around.

Clattering down the road towards the bridge was a chariot drawn by a single horse. Beefy held the reins. Beside him, Reedy was pointing at Livia, who stood frozen.

'Quick!' Felix urged. 'It's the governor's men.'

Spurred into action, Livia began to run.

Reedy called in his high voice, 'Stop her! Guards – seize that girl!'

The soldiers guarding the gate raised their spears and advanced.

'This way, Livia,' yelled Felix, quickening his pace. His mind, too, was racing. A girl was herding some geese across the bridge, followed by a trio of chattering women with baskets full of onions and turnips. Perhaps Felix and Livia could mingle among them, so the soldiers didn't know who it was they were meant to be stopping.

He looked over his shoulder to see the chariot overtake Livia and swerve into her path. Reedy leaped nimbly off the back and moved behind her to block the possibility of retreat.

'Livia!' Felix attempted to run back the way he had come, only to trip over the chicken.

'Thought you'd got away, didn't you?' crowed Reedy.

'Please,' begged Livia in a voice quite unlike her usual haughty tone. 'Don't take me back there.'

'Quiet,' thundered Beefy.

Felix, sprawled on the ground, watched in shock as the governor's men grabbed Livia roughly and tied her wrists behind her back. When she opened her mouth to scream, Reedy stuffed a gag in it.

As Felix scrambled to his feet, Beefy half dragged, half carried her to the chariot and shoved her in, then he and Reedy climbed up after her.

With a flick of the reins, Beefy turned the horse about. As the chariot wheeled around, Felix caught a glimpse of Livia's face gazing at him from where she was slumped on the floor by the men's feet. Her eyes were wide with terror.

Felix stood on the bridge for a long time, watching as the chariot grew smaller in the distance. He kept watching until it was no longer in sight.

'I'm hungry,' said the chicken.

Felix realised he was too: hungry and hopeless. He had no money, no food, no transport. All he had was a sacred chicken, and that didn't seem to be bringing him much good fortune. He'd had no plan for getting to Rome when he ran away, but that hadn't seemed to matter when he was with Livia. She had seemed so brave and determined that it had made Felix feel confident too.

But she was on her way back to the governor's mansion. It was just him and the chicken now. His most immediate concern, he decided, was their next meal. It would be easier to work out how to get to Rome if he wasn't so hungry.

He walked through the town gates unchallenged, and found himself on a busy street lined with two-storey buildings. The shops on the ground floor were selling everything from shoes made of leather to copper cooking pots. He passed a baker's stall set out under the cover of an overhanging balcony and looked longingly at the loaves stacked neatly on a wooden bench. Reaching a crossroads, he saw a tavern on the nearest corner. Above the door was a sign painted with a golden cockerel. 'That has to be a good omen,' he said to the chicken. He stepped inside only to be shooed out immediately by a woman wielding a broom.

'I'm looking for work,' Felix said politely. 'I'd be happy to do the sweeping for you. I just need a few coins.'

The woman brayed a laugh. 'I couldn't have you in here; you'd scare away the customers. You look like a beastie. Though I don't know how many beasties travel with a chicken.'

That was a bit rude, Felix thought. Clearly the woman didn't like redheaded boys.

Felix headed down a narrow alley away from the bustle. Perhaps in a quiet, out-of-the-way tavern they would be more inclined to help redheaded runaways with chickens.

But the alleyway didn't produce any such taverns, only a few quiet, out-of-the-way houses with blank white walls and small windows. At the end of the alley was a square with a water trough in its centre. Walking over to it, he gazed at his reflection in the water's surface. The boy staring back was so covered in mud and leaves and chicken feathers he was barely recognisable as Felix. He was extremely dusty and dirty, and there was no sign of his red hair.

Felix had to admit the broom-wielding woman had a point. 'I do look a bit like a beastie,' he conceded as he took off his cloak and shook it out, then sluiced icy water over his head and scrubbed at spots on his tunic.

'You could wash too,' he told the chicken.

The chicken gave itself a shake but declined Felix's offer to dunk it in the trough. 'There's no need. My natural beauty will always shine through.'

When Felix was clean – or cleaner, at any rate – he walked back down the alley to the main street and continued on into the heart of the town, grateful that it wasn't raining and there was a chance the weak sun might dry his still-damp clothes.

After a few minutes he entered a market square. Although the stalls had long since been packed up, the chicken found a scattering of grain to peck at, complaining the whole time. Felix's own supper was two limp carrots that had clearly been considered rubbish.

The sun was setting, and rather than risk being found by the nightwatchmen, who might be on the alert for a boy and/or sacred chicken who'd deserted the army, they left the town before curfew. It had started to rain again, and they found shelter under the same bridge they had walked across with Livia only a couple of hours before. Where was she now? Felix wondered. Would her father punish her for running away, or would he be so relieved to see her home that he'd order a huge banquet in her honour, with ... what else did rich people eat besides baked dormice and roast peacock? Nightingale tongues? Boiled flamingo?

He rubbed his empty stomach ruefully. Tomorrow, he vowed, he would make a plan to get himself and the chicken a good meal *and* passage to Rome. And he would try to forget Livia's scared eyes ...

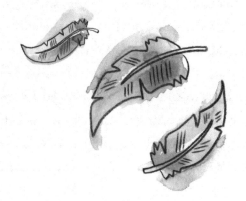

Chapter 5

Felix spent the morning in and around Durocortorum, trying to make some money. He earned a few coins shovelling manure in the stables of an inn. He earned another holding a horse for a well-dressed man while he heeded the call of nature. He earned a whole handful when he helped unload some amphorae of wine from a boat that had come by river from Lutetia. After the jars had been arranged in the back of the cart, he rode with the delivery driver to help unload the wine at a tavern just outside town. Felix recognised it as one they had walked past the day before.

'This wine has come all the way from Rome, you know,' said the delivery driver as they ferried the amphorae from the cart to the tavern's cellar. 'There are merchants over west in Lutetia who import it and then ship it all over Gaul.'

It cheered Felix to know that the clay containers were from Rome; it made him feel a little bit closer to home.

When they were done, the man said, 'Well, thanks for your help. Do you and your chicken want a lift back to town?'

Felix considered this, then decided that while he was here he might as well ask the tavern owners if they had any odd jobs that needed doing.

'No thanks,' he said to the driver. 'We'll stay here.'

'Okay,' said the man with a shrug. 'Er, do you take your chicken with you everywhere you go?'

'I have to,' Felix said. 'He's—' He stopped, realising how odd it would seem to be travelling with a sacred chicken. The man might think he'd stolen it. He finished, 'He's my friend. And I've promised to take him to Rome.'

The delivery driver gave him an odd look along with a handful of coins.

As he counted the money he'd collected that morning, Felix wondered how long it would take him to earn enough for a seat in a carriage. Or two seats, if the chicken insisted on having its own. It would probably take a lot more than eleven coins.

He was about to enter the tavern when the sound of hooves made him turn. Two men were pulling up in a chariot. Perhaps he should offer to hold their horse? He had started towards them when, with a shock of recognition, he drew back.

'It's the governor's men,' he whispered to the chicken.

'Who?' said the chicken, scratching at the dirt in an uninterested way.

'Beefy and Reedy – the ones who caught Livia.'

'Who?' said the chicken again.

Felix sighed. 'Never mind. I'm going to follow them and see if I can find out what happened to her. You wait here.'

He entered the tavern. It was dim inside – dim enough that he doubted the two men would recognise him if he slipped past them without a word. Maybe he could find a quiet corner nearby in which to stand and eavesdrop on their conversation.

The governor's men had seated themselves on benches on either side of a wooden table. Felix was preparing to slip past when one of them gestured to him.

'You, boy,' said Beefy.

Uh-oh – had they recognised him? Would he be in trouble with the governor for helping Livia?

But Beefy hardly spared him a glance. He just clicked his sausage-like fingers and said, 'Fetch us some ale.'

Felix looked around. He was the only boy in sight. 'Who, me?'

'It's your job, isn't it?'

'Uh … yes! Yes, it is!' Felix said, realising that this was his chance to find out what had happened to Livia without having to lurk in dusty corners.

Approaching the counter, he said to the innkeeper, 'The men at the table near the door would like two tankards of ale. I can carry them over for you, if you'd like.'

When Felix returned with the ale, Beefy took a long drink, which he followed with a long belch. He squinted at Felix and said, 'You seem familiar. Have we met before?'

'I don't think so,' said Felix, hoping his voice didn't sound too nervous.

'You're thinking of that boy we saw in the forest with his chicken,' Reedy piped up. 'There's a bit of a resemblance, but this boy has red hair; the other one had hair the colour of mud.'

Keen to change the subject, Felix said, 'Is that your chariot parked outside?'

Beefy took another big slurp of his ale, burped and nodded.

'It's a beauty!' Felix enthused. 'You must be pretty important to have a chariot like that.'

Beefy puffed out his chest. 'We've been on a mission for the governor of Nemetacum.'

'Wow, you've come all the way from Nemetacum? I could have sworn I saw you driving past yesterday. I always notice the finest chariots. Surely you can't have gone all the way to Nemetacum and back in that time.'

'Ha – we're fast but not that fast. We've been to Noviodunum though.'

'And we're hungry,' added Reedy. 'What are today's specials?'

'What took you to Noviodunum?' asked Felix, ignoring Reedy's question.

Beefy wiped the moustache of beer foam from his upper lip. 'We brought in a runaway, delivered her to the prefect. They'll keep her there till the governor's steward arrives from Nemetacum to take her back.'

'Oh, right,' said Felix casually. 'I heard the governor's daughter was missing. Livia, was that her name?'

Beefy gave a short laugh. 'The governor has a daughter called Livia all right, but it wasn't her that was missing.'

'It was her slave,' Reedy chipped in. 'Ran off in the night – took all her mistress's jewels too.'

For a moment Felix couldn't speak; he was struggling to make sense of the men's words. 'The runaway you captured was a *slave?*'

He felt a slow burn building inside his chest. It was fury, he realised.

Turning on his heel, he headed for the door.

'Hey, boy, where are you going?' Beefy called after him. 'I want another ale.'

'And I want something to eat,' Reedy reminded him.

Felix kept walking. The blood was boiling in his head. *How dare she?* All that hoity-toity attitude. The scornful way she talked to him. When all along she was nothing but a lowly slave. A slave *and* a thief!

The grand house she'd hinted at? She'd lived in that house as a slave! She'd probably never eaten a dormouse in her life.

To think he'd been polite to her. Almost in awe of her!

Storming out of the tavern, he kicked a bucket and sent it clattering across the stones. What a fool she must have thought him.

As if to prove her right, he promptly tripped over the bucket he'd kicked and fell face-first into a puddle.

Dripping, muddy and angrier than ever, he stalked over to where the sacred chicken sat in Beefy and Reedy's chariot.

'Come on,' said Felix. 'We're leaving.'

'I'm tired of walking,' the chicken said. 'Let's take this chariot.'

'We can't do that – it's not ours to take.'

It had taken Livia away, though …

Hmph, he thought, kicking one of the chariot's wooden wheels. She'd probably been laughing to herself the whole time.

Though she didn't laugh often, now that he thought about it. She was mostly quiet and serious and determined to the point of bossiness. It had made those rare times when she did laugh all the more special. And she was generous, he reminded himself. She had shared her bread with him and the chicken. Even if those jewels in her basket were stolen, she hadn't hesitated to suggest using them to buy passage to Rome for him as well as herself when they got to Durocortorum.

He closed his eyes, trying to banish the memory of his last sight of her, bound and gagged at the bottom of the chariot. The broken voice in which she'd begged, *Please*.

When he opened his eyes, he found to his surprise that he was standing in the chariot.

He picked up the horse's reins.

A voice from behind yelled, 'Hey! What are you doing? That's our chariot!'

Turning, he saw Beefy and Reedy advancing towards him.

'It's the boy from the forest,' shrieked Reedy. 'The one with mud-coloured hair and a chicken. I knew I recognised him!'

As he'd seen Beefy do the day before, Felix flicked the reins.

At once, the horse set off towards the road at a trot.

'We'll be in Rome in no time,' said the chicken happily.

'Stop!' thundered Beefy.

Felix flicked the reins again, harder this time, urging the horse into a canter as they joined the road.

But instead of turning south towards Rome, he turned north.

'Wait,' said the chicken as they clattered along the flagstones. 'Where are we going? I thought Rome was the other way.'

'We're not going to Rome yet,' Felix said grimly. 'First we're going to rescue Livia.'

Chapter 6

It was late afternoon when they arrived in Noviodunum. Caesar had won a battle here, Felix remembered, not long before the Battle of Gergovia – one of the rare battles Caesar had lost …

He stopped at a sausage stall by the side of the road. 'I have a message to deliver to the prefect,' he told the sausage seller, trying to sound important. (The delicious smell of sizzling sausages was very distracting.) 'Could you direct me to his house, please?'

The sausage seller looked at Felix and then the chicken, which was napping beside him.

'Do you always travel with a chicken?'

'Uh, yes,' Felix replied. 'It's a sacred chicken. It … it brings me good fortune.'

The sausage seller raised his eyebrows. 'If you say so.'

'Sorry to rush you,' Felix said, casting an anxious glance over his shoulder, 'but I'm in a bit of a hurry.'

'Urgent message, is it?' said the sausage man. He turned the sausages on the grill one at a time before saying, 'Now, what was it you wanted? Oh yes, the prefect's house. Well, you head straight—' He stopped. 'There's something wrong with your nose.'

'Huh?' Putting a hand to his nose, Felix realised it was twitching. 'Sorry,' he said. 'It's been a while since I ate. Perhaps I could have one of those …'

'If I were you I'd eat the chicken,' the sausage seller advised. He held out a sausage, waving away Felix's meagre handful of proffered coins, and described the route Felix should take.

As he ate, Felix urged the horse into a walk and, following the sausage seller's instructions, headed towards the centre of town, past warehouses and workshops and small houses, before reaching a street of larger houses snaking off to the left. The largest house of all belonged to the prefect. Felix would have recognised it even without the sausage man's description. Unlike the structures of timber and thatch around it, the prefect's house looked Roman, built of stone and brick.

As Felix slowed the horse to a stop outside, the chicken woke up. 'Where are we?' it asked.

'The prefect's house,' Felix replied.

'I'm coming in with you,' the chicken announced. 'This looks like the kind of place that has cake.'

'We're not here for cake,' Felix said. 'We're here to rescue Livia.'

'Who?' said the chicken.

'The question is,' Felix muttered to himself, ignoring the chicken, 'how will we find her?'

He directed the horse to follow the wall enclosing the house and garden to the back entrance, where deliveries were made.

'Stay here,' he told the chicken, 'and keep quiet.'

He left the chariot under a tree and pushed tentatively at the big wooden gate set in the wall, hoping he might be able to pass through unnoticed. Unfortunately the gate was locked.

He scanned the wall, looking for handholds and toeholds, but it was too smooth to climb. Frustrated, he walked back to the chariot and sat down. *Think!* he urged himself. There must be a way to get in.

Glancing up at the tree under which he'd parked, Felix saw that the lower branches brushed the top of the wall. *Aha!* He stood and carefully stepped up onto the edge of the chariot. Then he reached over his head and grasped a bough. He heaved himself onto the branch and slid along it until he had a view over the wall into a cobbled courtyard.

The afternoon light had faded into dusk, and his view was slightly obscured by leaves, making it hard at first to get his bearings, though he thought he could make out stables on the far side of the yard from the back door of the house. He could hear chickens clucking and squawking, too, though he couldn't see them. He only hoped the sacred chicken wouldn't feel compelled to join in.

As he watched the yard, the back door opened and a slender woman in a plain tunic stepped out to empty a bucket of water. Behind her, Felix saw a kitchen hearth.

He waited a few minutes then, when all was quiet, he lowered himself from the branch to the top of the wall, teetered for a moment, and jumped down into the courtyard.

He landed heavily. 'Ooph!'

'Who's there?'

The kitchen door opened and someone stepped outside with a lantern.

Felix, trapped in the middle of the courtyard with nowhere to hide, froze.

The lantern was raised, catching Felix in its circle of light. It was the woman he'd seen earlier – a kitchen slave, he presumed.

'What is it, Sulpicia?' a man's voice called from inside.

Felix opened his eyes wide, silently begging the woman not to cry out.

The woman frowned, opened her mouth.

Felix's legs began to shake.

'There's nothing here,' she called. 'Only the rooster, making a nuisance of himself as usual.' As she said it, she was pointing towards the stable across the courtyard. Was that where the rooster was?

'But I heard an *ooooph*,' the man inside objected. 'Roosters don't go *ooooph*.' His voice was getting closer.

The woman jabbed her finger towards the stable and finally Felix realised that she was signalling to him to go there – and fast.

As the kitchen door edged open, he dashed across the courtyard. By the door of the stable he could make out a pile of hay and he promptly threw himself into it.

'By Saturn, did you see that flash of red? The rooster ran away fast enough when he saw me coming! He knows who's boss, that's for sure. Strange though—'

the man's voice was getting fainter now '—I've never heard a rooster go *ooooph* before. Are you coming?'

'In a minute,' the woman replied. 'I just want to make sure the hens are all right.'

Felix lay in the hay waiting for his heart to stop pounding. He could hear horses whinnying softly and a cat mewing close by.

After a moment he stood up, brushed the hay from his hair and clothes, and waited for his eyes to adjust to the gloom. The cat was still mewing; it sounded like it was coming from the first stall.

Peering in, he saw the cat curled up on the earth floor ... But no – it was too big to be a cat.

Livia!

Just as when he'd seen her last, there was a cloth stuffed in her mouth as a gag and her hands and legs were tied.

He dropped to his knees next to her. She looked at him, eyes wild and scared.

He pulled the cloth from her mouth and she drew a few deep, ragged breaths.

'Felix!' she gasped, when she could speak again. 'How did you—?'

'I'll explain later. We have to get out of here.'

He began to struggle with the rope binding her hands. But it was no good. The knot was too tight and haste was making his fingers clumsy. 'I can't do it,' he said, frustrated. 'I'll have to carry you, and we'll try to find a knife later.'

'Here.'

A soft voice from behind startled him. Turning, he saw it was the woman from the kitchen.

She pressed a knife into Felix's hand. 'Be quick.'

Felix sawed desperately at the rope binding Livia's hands while their saviour used nimble fingers on the knot binding her feet.

'Thank you,' Livia said in a croaky voice.

The pair of them helped Livia up. After the hours she'd spent tied up, she could barely stand.

'This way,' the woman whispered. 'Quickly. We'll all be in trouble if the steward catches us.'

Felix draped one of Livia's arms over his shoulders and, with an arm encircling her waist, helped her across the courtyard behind the kitchen slave.

'Sulpicia, where are you?'

'Coming!'

Rather than crossing the courtyard to the gate, Sulpicia led them around the side of the stable to a door set in the wall. She opened it and ushered them through.

'I saw those men bringing her here,' she told Felix. 'She was kicking and scratching like a wild cat, she was that desperate. Sobbing about an arena in Rome and lions. It sounds like they must be planning something dreadful for her. I'm glad you found her.'

The woman was taking a terrible risk by helping them. Felix hoped suspicion wouldn't fall on her when it was discovered Livia was gone.

'How did you get here?' Livia asked him in a weak voice as the woman silently closed the door behind them.

'I stole a chariot.' In the dusky light, Felix led her along the wall enclosing the courtyard until he could just make out the shape of the tree under which he'd parked.

Livia gave a faint laugh that turned into a cough.

'Where's the chicken?' she asked.

'I left it with the chariot. I hope it's still there.'

'The chicken or the chariot?'

'Both, of course.'

'The chariot would be more useful.'

Though offended on the sacred chicken's behalf, Felix was reassured. Despite her ordeal, Livia had lost none of her spirit.

To Felix's relief, the chariot was where he had left it, and the sacred chicken was too.

'You're still here,' Livia said to it, sounding less than relieved.

'Oh, it's you,' said the chicken.

'Let's go,' said Felix.

The horse seemed to remember the way, and was soon walking briskly back along the road through town. Felix was longing to go faster, but thought it better not to attract attention.

'I still don't understand how you found me,' Livia said as they clopped past the sausage seller.

Felix explained how he had encountered Livia's captors in the inn. 'They said …' He paused, not sure how to broach the subject. 'They said that you're a slave.'

For a long moment, Livia didn't respond, just stared straight ahead. Her face was fixed in a frown. At last she said defiantly, 'I *was* a slave, but I'm not anymore.'

Felix glanced at her. 'I don't think you can just decide that for yourself.'

Livia crossed her arms. 'I don't see why not. What gives anyone the right to own me?'

Felix wasn't sure how to answer that question. He presumed Livia's parents had been captured in a battle, brought to Rome and sold at the slave market. Which was what would have happened to him if he'd fallen into the hands of the Nervians thanks to General Porcius's bad luck.

'How would you like it if you were made a slave through no fault of your own?' Livia continued, as if she knew what he was thinking.

He wouldn't like it at all, Felix admitted to himself. Was Livia running away from the governor any different from him running away from the Nervians if he'd been captured? He had an uncomfortable feeling that his situation and Livia's were somewhat alike.

'Why didn't you tell me earlier that you were a slave?' he asked, instead of answering her question.

Livia fixed him with a penetrating gaze. 'If I'd told you when we first met, what would you have done? Would you have let me go with you?'

Felix blushed. 'No,' he confessed. 'I would've thought you were bad for running away.'

'And now that you know the truth, are you going to turn me in?' she demanded.

'Of course not!' he replied. 'I just rescued you, didn't I?'

To his surprise, she beamed at him. 'You did. Thank you.'

She reminded him of his sisters. Perhaps it was the same with any slave – they were all just people like him and his family? It troubled him that he hadn't considered this before.

'Livia,' he began. Then it occurred to him that Livia wasn't her real name; it was the name of the governor's daughter. 'What should I call you?' he asked.

She gave him a puzzled look. 'You know my name.'

'But Livia's not *your* name. Those men told me that Livia's the name of your mistress. I mean your *true* name – the one you were born with.'

Livia bit her lip and glanced away. When she turned back he thought he saw a glint of tears in her eyes. 'I don't know what name my parents gave me. I can't ... I can't even remember them. For as long as I can remember I've been Livia's. Like those men said, I belong – belonged – to Livia. All anyone has ever called me was Livia's: Livia's slave, Livia's girl, until Livia became my name too.'

Felix gaped at her. He didn't know what to say. She didn't even have a name of her own.

She shrugged then smiled shyly. 'But when you call me Livia it sounds like my real name.'

The sight of her smile made a smile tug at his own lips. 'Okay, Livia – let's get a move on.' As Felix lifted the reins, he realised he didn't know which direction they should go. He couldn't take her to Rome; Sulpicia at the prefect's house had said Livia was scared of being sent to the arena. Maybe she'd like to return to her real home, the place where her parents had come from – wherever that was. 'Um, where would you like to go?'

'Rome,' Livia said promptly. 'As quickly as possible.'

'Are you sure?' he asked doubtfully. It didn't make sense – surely she should be running as far from Rome as possible if she was going to be sent to the lions?

'Hurry!' she said. 'Before the prefect notices I've gone.'

Whichever way they were headed, hurrying seemed like a very good idea. They were nearing the outskirts of the town now; he could see the Durocortorum road ahead. As they turned onto the flagstones Felix urged the horse into a gallop.

Felix and Livia clung to the edge of the carriage, but the chicken was flung about from side to side.

'This is no way to travel,' it muttered crossly. 'Why do we have to go so fast?'

Felix was about to say that the prefect's men might be behind them, when it occurred to him that Beefy and Reedy would be coming towards them from Durocortorum. He glanced behind for the prefect's men then peered at the road in front for the governor's men. Behind, then in front. Behind, then in front. Before long the constant swivelling of his head to look for pursuers was making him dizzy.

What would the general do if the enemy attacked from more than one direction? Felix asked himself. He thought longingly of the tortoise formation, and how the soldiers to the front and sides locked shields, while those in the centre held their shields over their heads to create an impenetrable barrier.

He, Livia and the sacred chicken had no hope of forming an impenetrable barrier. What other strategies did the general use? He thought of General Porcius poring over the map, studying the terrain. That's what he'd have to do too: use the terrain to their advantage and take a path their pursuers weren't expecting. Instead of going by carriage from Durocortorum, as they'd originally planned, they had to find another way to get to Rome.

He was reminded of the delivery driver he'd helped that morning, the one who'd talked of how wine from Rome was imported to Lutetia and then sent all over Gaul. If wine could travel from Rome to Lutetia, couldn't he, Livia and the sacred chicken make the reverse journey?

After another quick glance behind and ahead, Felix tugged on the reins to slow the horse. 'I've got an idea,' he said. 'One that will throw everyone off our trail. We need to go west.' Quickly, he explained about Lutetia.

'That sounds good to me,' Livia said. 'I don't care which way we go, so long as we get to Rome.'

'And I don't care which way we go,' the sacred chicken added, 'so long as it isn't by chariot. Perhaps a carriage of some sort …'

'That's not exactly what I had in mind,' Felix said as he steered the horse and chariot to the side of the road and stepped down.

Fingers fumbling with the knots in the dark, Felix hastily unhitched the horse from the chariot. 'Now help me push the chariot into the ditch so no one can tell what path we've taken,' he said to Livia. 'Then we'll ride the horse through the forest.'

Together they shoved the chariot into the ditch.

'I'll get on first,' Felix said, approaching the horse.

Livia put her hands on her hips. 'Why should you be in front?'

You'd never know he'd rescued her only hours ago – or that she had ever been a slave. She was as bossy as ever.

'Have you ever ridden a horse?' Felix retorted.

'No. Have *you*?'

'No,' Felix admitted. 'But the horse and I have developed a bond.' He held out his hand to the horse, which promptly bit it. 'Ouch!' He snatched his hand back.

'Let me try,' said Livia.

Holding her palm out, she let the horse sniff it before stroking the velvety nose. Leaning close, she murmured in the horse's ear and then pulled back to look deep into its brown eyes. The horse snuffled softly.

'I think she prefers me,' Livia said, sounding just a little smug.

'Fine,' said Felix crossly. 'You go in front.'

He made a cradle of his hands for Livia to step on, and she leaped lightly onto the horse's back. After he'd passed the sacred chicken to her, Livia extended a hand to help him clamber up. Then, with the chicken wedged between Livia's back and Felix's front, they left the road for the shelter of the forest.

They rode through the night, the horse plodding through the trees, Livia occasionally adjusting their course when the moon deigned to show itself.

Felix, who'd been on edge since stealing the chariot that morning – could it really still be the same day? – finally felt some of the tension drain from his body. Before long he found himself drifting into a doze, lulled by the slow rhythm of the horse's gait, the muffled quiet of the forest ...

His slumber was broken abruptly by Livia's scream and the chicken's squawk.

Felix opened his eyes to see two men standing in their path brandishing knives.

The early-morning sun glinted off the blades as one of them barked, 'Hold it right there!'

Chapter 7

The bandits were alarming to behold: big, burly, bearded men who ran at them, roaring.

With a frightened neigh, the horse reared back, and its passengers tumbled to the ground.

'Give us all your valuables,' the black-bearded bandit ordered.

Felix was too winded from the fall to speak.

'Well?' the bandit said.

'We don't have any valuables,' Livia gasped.

'What about your jewels?' said the chicken.

'She doesn't have them anymore,' Felix hissed.

The blond-bearded bandit squinted at them suspiciously. 'Don't you have *anything* of value?'

'There's me,' the chicken declared. 'I am a sacred chicken! My value is beyond compare.'

'What's it squawking about?' the bandit asked.

'I think it's hungry,' Felix replied.

'This has been a waste of time,' Blond Beard grumbled, sticking his knife back in his belt.

'Wait,' said Black Beard. 'What about the horse?'

'Hmm,' said Blond Beard, considering. 'It's a fine-looking horse.'

Livia sprang to her feet. 'No,' she said, clutching the horse around the neck. 'We won't give her up.'

She didn't have half that much affection for the chicken, Felix noted, even though it was sacred and the horse wasn't.

'We're not asking you to give it up,' said Black Beard.

'Oh, good,' said Livia, sounding relieved.

'We're *telling* you!' He pulled the knife from his belt and advanced towards them, swishing the blade from side to side. 'Any objections?'

'No,' Felix squeaked. Livia shook her head, eyes wide.

They stood there, speechless, as the bandits mounted the horse and rode off in the direction of the sunrise.

When the sound of hooves had faded, Livia turned resolutely away. 'Let's go.' She began walking, her head down.

'Come on,' Felix said to the chicken.

'I don't feel so good,' the chicken complained.

'You're probably just feeling a bit queasy after being thrown from the horse.'

'No, it's not that,' said the chicken. 'I think it was something I ate.'

'You haven't eaten in ages,' said Felix. 'You must mean you're feeling hungry.'

'No, it was definitely something I ate. It must have been at the prefect's house.'

'What are you talking about?' said Felix. 'We didn't eat at the prefect's house.'

'I did.'

'What?!'

'Don't yell,' begged the chicken. 'I told you: I'm not feeling very well.' It swayed on its feet for a minute then let out a giant burp.

Something small and hard landed on Felix's foot.

'Yuck,' he said. 'What is it? A piece of gristle?' He peered down at it. He'd never known gristle to gleam before. 'Hang on – this is a gold ring.' He picked it up.

'Oh, is that what it was?' said the chicken. 'It looked shiny, so I ate it.'

'Wait, you ate this *where*?'

'I told you: at the prefect's house. You were gone such a long time and I started to get hungry, so I went inside to see if I could find something to eat.'

Felix rubbed his forehead. 'Let me get this straight,' he began, but was distracted by Livia, who was marching down the path towards them, eyes flashing.

'Will you two hurry up?'

'Sorry, the chicken wasn't feeling well. It swallowed this ring at the prefect's house and just burped it up.' He showed it to her.

Livia examined it. 'It's got a chicken engraved on it. What are the odds? The chicken burped up a chicken ring. I guess if it's valuable we might be able to use it. Now, come on – we're wasting time.' Her voice was sharp with impatience as she set off down the path again.

The ring was too loose for his fingers so Felix jammed it on his thumb, where it stuck tight. Then he and the chicken – who seemed to be feeling much better – hurried to catch up.

The loss of the horse to the bandits slowed their progress so much that Felix started to wonder if they would have been better off going to Durocortorum after all, despite the risks. For two days they tramped west through forests of conifers. The rain had stopped only for the snow to start, and the tall, dark trunks of the conifers were stark against the white-tipped leaves and forest floor. But although they were getting closer to Lutetia (surely!), Felix felt a growing sense of despair at the realisation that by travelling west rather than south, they were hardly any closer to Rome than when they'd started.

'Livia,' he said, 'can I ask you a question?'

Livia eyed him warily. 'I suppose.'

'Why did you suggest we travel together back when we first met?'

Livia shrugged. 'At first I just thought there'd be safety in numbers, and that it would be a good disguise. And I liked the fact that you seemed a bit in awe of me when you thought I was the daughter of a senator. No one had ever treated me like that before – with respect, I mean.' She gave him a sideways look. 'But I guess you feel differently now that you know the truth.'

Felix shook his head vigorously. 'No,' he said. 'You're wrong. I'm more in awe of you than before. Running away like that – you have more courage than I ever will.'

'You ran away too,' she reminded him.

'Yes, but … I'm going home. Why are *you* going to Rome?' *With the arena and the lions*, he thought.

There was a long pause, then she said, 'To see my brother.'

'What? You have a brother?'

But it seemed Livia was done answering questions. She picked up her pace so that Felix and the sacred chicken struggled to keep up.

They walked on. The forests gave way to fields, fields to small plots, small plots to small houses, and then all of a sudden they had crossed a bridge and were in Lutetia. Instead of trees there were basilicas and temples, baths and theatres, and people everywhere.

Felix scanned the street. One of the temples was particularly striking, not so much for the height of its dazzling white columns as for the flock of dazzling white birds at the building's base. 'Look,' he said. 'A flock of—'

'Geese!' cried the chicken, its beady eyes alight with pleasure. 'Such noble birds!'

Livia considered the waddling, squabbling rabble doubtfully. 'Really?'

'To be fair, the sacred geese of Juno *did* save Rome from invaders,' Felix said.

'A bunch of honking hooligans like this?' scoffed Livia. 'You're making it up.'

'I am not!' said Felix. 'It was when the Gauls were invading. They were trying to take the fortress on the top of Capitoline Hill in the middle of the night, but the sacred geese that lived in the Temple of Juno sounded the alarm and saved the day.'

'And when was this?' Livia wanted to know.

Felix shrugged. 'About three hundred and fifty years ago.'

'Well, it's a good story,' Livia conceded.

'I'm going to introduce myself,' said the chicken. 'It's only polite, as one sacred bird to another.' It let out an ear-splitting squawk.

The geese raised their heads.

'Squawk! Squawk!' the chicken called.

'Honk! Honk!' said the geese.

There was a further exchange of squawks and honks, and then the chicken cried, 'Cake! These geese are fed on cake! And they've invited me to join them.' It began to hurry away.

'Wait,' said Felix. 'What are you doing?'

'What does it look like?' the chicken asked over its shoulder. 'I'm leaving.'

'You're *leaving*?' Felix felt unexpectedly reluctant to let the chicken go. 'What about Rome? What about *us*?'

'Who?' the chicken said. Then it ran towards the other birds without a backwards glance and was soon lost from sight, one sacred chicken in a flock of sacred geese.

Livia put a hand on Felix's arm. 'If he wants to make a goose of himself we can't stop him.'

Felix sighed. 'I suppose you're right. What now?'

'We keep going to Rome, of course.'

Chapter 8

Felix's impression of Lutetia was of a lively, bustling town, but he didn't have much of a chance to take it in as Livia set off at a fast pace.

'I hope the sacred chicken will be okay,' he fretted, looking back towards the temple where they'd left their friend. At least, Felix had considered the chicken a friend – a careless, complaining kind of friend.

Livia tossed her head. 'I'll never understand why you're so attached to that haughty, bossy bird.'

Perhaps you needed to be in the military to understand the power of the sacred chicken, Felix mused.

'Come *on*,' she said, gesturing for Felix to keep up.

'It's okay,' Felix said. 'I'm pretty sure we're safe. The governor would never think to look for you here.'

'It's not that,' said Livia. She bit her lip. 'There's something I haven't told you.'

Felix felt a flicker of alarm. 'There's someone else chasing us?'

'No – I hope not. But I need to get to Rome fast.'

'I don't understand what the hurry is,' said Felix. 'I thought you just needed to get away from the governor's house. What's in Rome?'

'My brother.'

'Why is it so important that you see your brother?'

'Because Julius Caesar is going to kill him!'

Felix's flicker of alarm became a flame. 'Caesar is going to kill your brother?!'

'Well, not with his own hands. He'll have my brother torn to pieces in the arena by a savage animal. Like a lion, or … or … an ostrich.'

Felix had never seen an ostrich, but he knew it was some kind of giant bird – and clearly a vicious one if it was used in the gladiator games.

'Caesar is going to make an ostrich kill your brother? Why?'

'Because of me!'

Felix was now struggling to keep up with both her pace *and* her story.

'What have *you* done to Caesar?'

'Nothing! It's just ...' She stopped walking abruptly and rubbed her eyes with the heels of her hands. 'Although we can't remember our parents,' she explained, her voice subdued, 'my brother and I have always been in the same household. When he heard that I'd be going to Gaul and he was to be left behind, he decided to steal a horse and come after me. He caught up to us near Mediolanum, but the governor's steward saw him. I told him not to follow us, that it was too dangerous! I don't know *why* he has to be so stubborn and headstrong.' She shook her head in frustration.

Felix decided not to point out that it might run in the family.

'Anyway,' she continued, 'the governor was furious. He sent my brother back to Rome in chains with orders that he be sent to the dungeon. Then, not long before I met you in the forest, a visitor from Rome told the governor that there's to be a series of triumphs in the first two weeks of April celebrating Caesar's victories and conquests. In the middle of the month, there'll be a special day of games. All the prisoners from the dungeon are going to be made to fight wild beasts in the arena! The Ides of April is only three months away. I need to be there. I have to save my brother ... or ... or at least say goodbye.' Her voice quavered.

That explained her desperate hurry. 'Okay,' Felix said, 'so what's the fastest way to Rome?'

'I don't know.'

Felix was struck by her tone of despair.

'That's all right,' he told her with more confidence than he felt. 'We'll find out.'

'How?'

'We need to talk to a wine merchant,' Felix said, remembering why he'd brought them to Lutetia. 'Someone who trades with Rome. They'll know all the quickest routes.'

Livia looked at him with something approaching admiration.

'And if we're looking for someone who does business,' Felix concluded, 'he'll probably be in the forum.'

The forum proved easy to find. The road they were on crossed another bridge and climbed a hill, and at the top was a large open space crowded with market stalls and surrounded by grand buildings.

Felix approached a group of men standing on the steps of the temple in the forum's centre. 'I'm looking for a wine merchant,' he said.

'And what do you need that for, lad?' asked one of the men. 'You own a tavern, do you?'

His fellows laughed.

'No,' said Felix, 'but I work for General Fabius Maximus Porcius, whose legion is in Belgica. He's sick of Belgian beer and he wants some wine imported from Rome.'

'A Roman general, eh? He'll be wanting the good stuff. In that case, you need to speak to Vino Vicarius. You'll find him eating in the Fattened Boar.'

'He *is* a bore!' chimed in another, and they all laughed some more.

Following the men's directions, Felix and Livia walked along a narrow street until they saw a wooden sign with a boar painted on it.

Inside the tavern were a couple of skinny men standing by the bar with tankards in front of them. Sitting by himself at a long table was a man with a tunic straining over his belly and what appeared to be the whole hindquarter of a roasted boar on a platter in front of him.

'That must be him,' Livia whispered.

Felix took a deep breath, then approached the bore with the boar. Coughing politely to get the man's attention, he said, 'Excuse me, sir ...'

The merchant put down the bone he was gnawing on and drew his eyebrows together.

'What's that?' he barked. 'Are you talking to me?'

'Er, my sister and I need to get back to Rome quickly for … for family reasons. We've heard in the forum that you do a lot of important business with Rome and know more than anyone in Lutetia about the best routes.'

The flattery worked. The merchant licked his fingers thoughtfully then said, 'If I were you, I'd take a fast carriage to Lugdunum and from there board a boat heading south to the sea. Get passage on a boat from Massilia to the port of Ostia. From Ostia it's only fifteen miles to Rome. You should be able to complete the whole journey inside a month. Of course, that's assuming you can afford it.'

He looked them up and down, and Felix was uncomfortably aware of how they must present: he was muddy, and Livia's tunic was torn and dirty.

'What would be the cheapest way?' he asked.

'Do the whole thing by road. On foot, it'll probably take three months or more.'

Livia frowned. 'That's too slow,' she said.

'If we walked as far as Lugdunum, maybe we could work for our passage aboard a boat from there to the coast,' Felix suggested.

'Someone might take you on, lad, but no one's going to give work to a girl.'

And that, it seemed, was that.

'It makes me so angry,' Livia said as they left the tavern. 'No one had any trouble making me work when I was a slave. I can work as hard as any boy. But if I'm not a slave they won't let me work because I'm a girl.' She kicked at a stone in frustration. 'It doesn't make sense!'

She was right, Felix thought. Spending time with Livia was making him question everything he'd thought he knew. Next, he'd even be questioning whether chickens really could be sacred! (No, he told himself. That was going too far.)

Within a few minutes they were back among the market stalls of the forum. Livia was staring at a stall where a barber was shaving a customer.

Before Felix could ask why, she was marching over. 'I need a haircut,' she announced.

The barber, surprised, jumped slightly and his customer cried out.

'See what you made me do,' the barber said crossly as he dabbed at the spot of blood on his customer's chin. 'We're all done here,' he added to the customer, who leaped from the chair like he'd had a narrow escape.

'Anyway, I don't cut girls' hair,' the barber said.

'Just as well,' Livia retorted, unperturbed, 'because I don't want a girl's haircut. I want you to cut my hair so it looks like his.' She pointed at Felix.

The barber looked at Felix then back at Livia. 'Are you sure?'

Livia looked at Felix too, and wrinkled her nose. 'Well, maybe not exactly like his. But as short as a boy's.'

What was wrong with his hair? Felix wondered. He ran a hand through it and dislodged several leaves and a dead beetle.

'We don't have much money,' Livia confessed.

The barber sighed. 'I suppose if you were to sweep my stall and sharpen my blades ...'

'Felix can do that while you cut,' Livia said. 'We're in a bit of a hurry.'

So Felix sharpened the barber's blades on a whetstone and swept, and the barber clipped Livia's long, dark hair. When he was done, he stood back.

Livia reached a hand up to the nape of her neck. 'It's very short,' she said, seeming self-conscious all of a sudden.

'That's what you asked for.'

The barber held up a hand mirror.

Livia gave a single nod then held out her hand. 'May I borrow your scissors, please?'

'If you cut off any more you'll be bald,' the barber protested.

'It's not for my hair.' Taking the scissors, she carefully cut her long tunic so that it came to just above her knees.

When she was done, she turned to Felix. 'Do I look like a boy?' she asked.

Felix considered her critically. Her features seemed finer than his somehow, and her limbs more slender, her knees not as knobbly. But if he didn't know she was a girl to start with, he might be fooled. 'Kind of,' he said.

She turned to the barber. 'Thank you. Now, where's the road to Lugdunum?'

Chapter 9

Felix closed his eyes against the brightness then opened them again. His overwhelming impression of the southern port of Massilia was that it was dazzling, with light reflecting off the sea, light reflecting off the white buildings. It was especially startling after so long spent in the grey and gloomy north of Gaul.

They'd made it here in record time. For two weeks they'd walked. When the coins Felix had earned in Durocortorum ran out they did odd jobs in exchange for food from farmhouses, taverns and market stalls. In Lugdunum they'd found a river galley transporting empty barrels made of oak to Massilia, where they would be filled with garum – the pungent fish oil used to flavour dishes from Rome to Germania – and sent to all parts of the world. Felix and his 'brother' had been taken on as oarsmen for the week-long journey. His brother, it had been noted, was by far the more skilled rower.

Felix rubbed his aching biceps ruefully and glanced at Livia. She was watching the quay for the return of the river captain, who had promised to put in a good word for them with the captain of the ship taking the barrels to Ostia.

For now, though, Felix was content to bask in the sun on the steps of a warehouse by the quay, as the bustle of the port carried on around them. Ships sailed from here to Greece, Hispania and Egypt, making it one of the busiest ports on the sea. A cart with clay jars clattered past, followed by a man wheeling a barrow stacked with glossy red bowls from a pottery workshop. The stink of salted fish wafted from the cluster of stalls that made up the fish market, alive with cries as the stallholders competed for attention.

'Get some mullet in yer gullet!' bawled one vendor.

'Get some cod in yer gob,' bellowed his rival.

'That doesn't even rhyme,' the first vendor pointed out.

'I know,' the rival confessed.

Felix called, 'Get some cod in your bod.'

Both vendors looked over. 'Not bad,' said the first. 'Give us another.'

Felix thought for a moment. 'Put some skate on your plate!' he suggested.

'Kid's got a way with words,' the second vendor observed. 'Got anything to rhyme with mackerel?'

At that moment, the river captain returned, saying, 'You're in luck – the *Tarshish* is in port. Come on, I'll introduce you to Captain Kanmi.'

The ship, he explained as they pushed through the crowd on the quay, would be sailing the next morning for Ostia. The crew was busy unloading oil lamps from Africa and taking on board the barrels of garum bound for Rome.

Their destination was the far end of the quay, where Felix saw a modest Phoenician merchant ship, long and narrow with eight oars to a side and a single broad sail attached to the sturdy mast. A horse's head was carved on the prow and watchful eyes were painted on either side of the bow.

The river captain herded Felix and Livia up the gangplank and along the deck to where the captain stood surveying the activity with watchful eyes. He had dark, curly hair and wore a long tunic tied with a bright blue sash.

'These are the lads I was telling you about. Hard workers – and cheap as they come.'

The watchful eyes were turned on Felix and Livia. 'Cheap, you say? How cheap?'

'We need to get to Rome as quickly as possible,' Felix explained. 'We're prepared to work for our passage without pay.'

The captain tugged at his beard. 'Well, the price is right. I suppose I could do with a couple more oarsmen.'

Not more rowing! Felix groaned inwardly. But Livia flexed her muscles and said, 'No problem. We love rowing.'

The captain looked dubious. 'This isn't some nice, calm river, you know – this is the sea, and we've five days of sailing ahead of us. I'd better put the pair of you on a single oar. In the meantime, you can give the crew a hand with the loading.'

After thanking the river captain for his help, Felix and Livia joined the rest of the crew ferrying vessels of garum along the dock and up the gangplank.

'Barrels over here, jugs over there!' roared the first mate, who was directing the loading.

'There's no need to shout,' said Livia over her shoulder as she rolled a barrel past him.

'What did you say?' The first mate seemed shocked.

Felix looked around the neck of the amphora he was carrying to explain. 'My brother doesn't like to be ordered around.'

'Doesn't like to be—? I'm the first mate! Giving orders is my job! *Your* job is to take them!'

'Not anymore it isn't,' said Livia. 'I am not your slave. I have entered into a business arrangement with your captain. I will carry and row, and he will take me to Ostia. Just think: a week from now I'll be in Rome!' And with that she gave the first mate a smile so dazzling that he forgot to shout orders for several minutes.

By the time the sun sank below the horizon, the boat was laden and all the crew were on board. Under the first mate's directions, they had stacked the cargo in the centre of the ship, between the rowing benches on the ship's port and starboard sides. Everything was in order for them to sail tomorrow.

The crew slept on the aft deck, and Felix was glad to stretch out and rest his weary limbs.

The boat was rocking gently on a slight swell, and Felix was almost asleep when he heard a squawk. He sighed. Would the sacred chicken never be quiet? 'Not now,' he mumbled.

To his relief, the chicken fell silent. The only sound was the creaking of timbers, the gentle lapping of water against the hull. He drifted towards sleep again.

Squawk!

Abruptly, Felix sat up. He'd heard it again – or dreamed it, rather. He must be missing the sacred chicken more than he'd realised.

A moment later, a voice said, 'Where's my cake?'

It was faint, carried on the wind, yet it was familiar. But it couldn't be!

'I told you,' replied a second voice wearily. 'I don't have any cake – just this grain.'

'But I don't *want* grain. I want cake.'

'Please,' the second voice begged. 'Eat the grain.'

'Won't.'

'Okay, okay. If I let the ship sail without us and I find you some cake, do you promise me everything will be all right?'

Moving quietly so as not to wake Livia, Felix rose, tiptoed to the rail of the ship and looked over the side.

The quay below was dark and quiet, and completely devoid of chickens, sacred or otherwise. It had been a dream after all.

He was about to head back to bed when he spied a dim light near the gangway. It must be the night watch, he presumed.

The light flashed then dimmed, flashed then dimmed again.

It was a signal, he realised, as the light flashed a third time.

From the darkness among the warehouses he saw a light flash three times in response.

As a figure slipped from the shadows, the person on the gangway held up his light. Felix recognised Captain Kanmi.

'Do you have it?' the captain asked in a hoarse whisper.

In answer, the cloaked figure held out what looked like a stick.

The captain took it in his hands and considered it almost reverently. 'So this is it, eh? Well, you'd better come aboard – we're sailing in a few hours.' He went to give the stick back but the cloaked figure held up his hand.

'There's been a change of plan,' he said gruffly. 'I need you to take this yourself and deliver it in my place. Someone will be there to meet the ship in Ostia. Tell him – tell him I was detained and will be following by road as quickly as possible. In the meantime, guard this with your life.'

'I'll keep it in my own cabin,' the captain promised, looking at the stick again. He seemed kind of dazed.

As the shadowy figure turned away, a gust of breeze blew his cloak aside and Felix saw that the man was wearing the uniform of a Roman general. Pulling the cloak tight, the man glanced around quickly. Felix ducked.

When he raised his head again to peer over the side, the man had disappeared.

The bobbing of the light along the gangway marked the captain's passage back onto the ship.

Then all was quiet. Felix crept back to his bed on the deck and lay down, puzzled by what he'd just seen. Why would a Roman general be down at the port in the dead of the night, giving sticks to the captain of a Phoenician merchant ship?

He was almost asleep when a second question occurred to him. Had the Roman general *really* been travelling with a chicken?

Chapter 10

They sailed at dawn the next day, Felix and Livia sharing a single oar.

As they left the harbour of Massilia and headed for open sea, the man on the oar in front turned and introduced himself as Hannibal.

'Like the great Carthaginian general?' Felix asked.

'No, like the elephant.'

Felix frowned. It was true the great general of Carthage was famed for the war elephants that marched with his army, but ... 'I thought Hannibal was the name of the general,' he said.

'Not according to my mother.'

Hannibal's head was a big bald dome, and his ears looked likely to flap in a strong breeze. He appeared as strong as an elephant, which proved to be the case when he rowed. While Felix and Livia strained at their oar, Hannibal's strokes were long and smooth.

Behind them sat a wiry man with a grey beard. His name was Gisgo, he said. 'The captain likes Hannibal for his strength and me for my seafaring knowledge,' he said. 'What's he got you two for?'

'Free,' said Felix. 'We're working for our passage.'

Gisgo raised his bushy grey eyebrows. 'The captain does like a bargain.' He watched them row for a moment before nodding at Livia. 'He got the better bargain with you, though. You've got a good style with the oar, lad.'

Livia opened her mouth to respond then closed it again, frowning.

'What is it?' said Gisgo. 'Did I say something wrong?'

Livia shook her head. 'It's just …' she began, and fell silent again.

'Just what, lad?' Gisgo prompted.

'I'm not a lad,' Livia blurted.

'Livia …' Felix cautioned.

'You're not a—' Gisgo turned to Felix. 'What does he mean?'

Felix shrugged.

'I'm a girl,' Livia said emphatically.

Gisgo gaped at her for a moment then turned his gaze to Felix. 'Is this true? Is your brother a girl?'

Felix had no idea how to answer this. 'He – I – she—' He gazed at Livia helplessly. 'Maybe?'

'I'm not his brother,' Livia clarified. 'And I'm ... I'm sick of pretending to be something I'm not.'

Hannibal glanced over his shoulder. 'You don't row like a girl,' he said.

'Oh yes I do,' Livia retorted. 'I'm a girl, and I'm rowing, so I must be rowing like a girl.'

Hannibal's face creased in bemusement. 'That means ... girls are good at rowing,' he said slowly.

'Exactly,' said Livia.

And it was just as well, Felix thought, as the sun beat down and they rowed and rowed and kept on rowing. He found the time passed more pleasantly if he forgot he was rowing and let his mind wander. The best distraction, though, was Gisgo, who told stories of the wonders he'd seen: sea monsters that could crush a ship in a single giant tentacle and mermaids bathing on rocks trying to lure sailors to their death. He described foreign ports and bazaars scented with exotic spices, where snake charmers tamed enormous serpents and magicians soared overhead on flying carpets.

Gisgo was relating a tale he'd heard in one such port, of a cave filled with treasure, when he caught sight of the ring glinting on Felix's thumb.

'Where's that from then?' he asked.

Felix exchanged a glance with Livia, who shook her head slightly in warning.

'It was our father's,' Felix said.

The greybeard shook his head. 'I still can't believe the two of you are related.'

'Felix was adopted,' Livia broke in.

Gisgo's gaze was still fixed on the ring. 'Is that a chicken engraved on it?'

'Our father was a chicken farmer,' said Livia.

'A chicken farmer with a gold ring?'

'Don't listen to her. I think she has a touch of sunstroke.' Felix was feeling a bit affected by the sun himself. Or was he affected by the number of stories he was trying to keep straight in his head? 'Our father was a general in the Roman army. And that's a sacred chicken on the ring.'

He was reminded of the mysterious general on the quay the night before. He must remember to tell Livia what he'd seen.

As the sun eased down the sky, throwing a golden cloak over the sea, the captain directed them to anchor in a calm cove. There they had an hour or two of leisure before dark. A couple of sailors fished off the deck, while others played dice games. One man did his laundry while another cut his fingernails. Then the second mate offered to teach Felix and Livia how to tie knots, and Felix forgot all about the scene on the quay.

On the fourth day the sea was the calmest it had been yet, the oars slipping easily through the water. Felix quite enjoyed the seafaring life. Now that he'd left the army he'd need a new career. Perhaps he could become a sailor?

By midday, he was less certain. There was a bright halo around the sun and the air wrapped around him like a damp sack. It was eerily silent, and he couldn't work out what was different at first. Then he realised that the birds that always seemed to be wheeling and diving around the ship were gone. 'Gisgo,' he called over his shoulder, 'what happened to all the birds?'

'I reckon they'll be heading for shore, lad. They're always the first to know.'

'The first to know what?' Livia asked.

'What's coming,' said Gisgo ominously.

Felix felt the shiver of a breeze against his face. Squinting into the glare, he saw high, wispy clouds scudding quickly across the sky. 'You mean like those clouds?' he asked, lifting a hand off the oar to point.

'It's the ones gathering on the horizon that'll cause the real trouble,' said Gisgo, directing Felix's attention to the tall banks of cloud in the distance. 'We could be in for a rough time.'

Felix's heart skipped a beat. 'How rough?'

'Ah, it's nothing to worry about, lad. See that horse's head on the prow? That's a tribute to Yamm, the Phoenician god of the sea. And those eyes on either side of the bow will see us through safely.'

Through what? Felix wondered, but he didn't quite like to ask.

As the afternoon passed, the wind strengthened, whipping up whitecaps on the sea's once-placid surface, and the captain ordered his men to lower the sail.

The sky grew dark, but unlike the tranquil twilight of the evening before, with stars twinkling above as the sailors had relaxed on deck, this was a menacing darkness. And with a chill, Felix recalled the warning he had overlooked …

'I've got a bad feeling, Livia,' he said in a low voice.

'I told you not to eat that squid,' she replied.

'It's not that. I saw an omen yesterday. I think we're headed for serious trouble.'

Usually Livia just rolled her eyes when he mentioned omens, but as the ship tilted and swayed in the swirling sea she looked at him in alarm. 'What about the horse's head on the prow and the eyes on the bow?' she demanded. 'I thought you said those things would protect us!'

'*I* didn't say it,' Felix reminded her. 'That was Gisgo. I don't know if they'll be enough to counteract what I saw the other day.' He drew a deep breath and turned to meet his friend's apprehensive gaze.

'What? What was it?' she said.

'There was a sailor cutting his fingernails when the sun was shining!'

For a second Livia just stared at him, her brow furrowed. Finally, she said, 'And?'

Felix gaped at her in disbelief. '*And* he should have known that it's bad luck to cut your hair or nails aboard a ship except during a storm!'

Even as he spoke, the wind began to howl, tossing the boat even more violently.

'Are you telling me that because a sailor cut his fingernails our ship is in trouble?' Livia yelled over the howling.

'I don't make the rules,' Felix shouted. 'But would it have hurt you to be nice to the sacred chicken?'

Livia gave him a perplexed look. 'What does the chicken have to do with anything?'

Felix shook his head. It was a good question. Why had the sacred chicken come to mind? 'I don't know,' he confessed. 'I thought I heard it in Massilia, the night before we set sail. It was asking for cake. And, well, I think we should have tried harder to find cake for it.'

Livia's eyes widened in outrage. 'You think that ridiculous chicken cursed us?'

Felix shrugged. 'Why else would it be haunting me?'

'I don't know … because you're strange?' Livia muttered. But she seemed frightened.

The sky was so dark now that Felix could no longer tell if it was day or night.

Waves were slamming into the ship, almost tipping it onto its side, and the deck was flooded with swirling water. The oarsmen had all abandoned their rowing. Big Hannibal had wedged himself beneath his bench and Gisgo was clinging like a limpet to his oar.

The sky was lit up momentarily by a flash of lightning, and to Felix's horror there was a terrible crack as it hit the mast.

'Livia, watch out!' Seizing Livia by the elbow, he dragged her from their bench and they ran aft as the mast teetered above them before crashing to the deck with a sound that echoed the boom of thunder now shaking the sky.

A giant wave swept over the starboard side, and Felix lost his grip on Livia's elbow. Before he could grab it again he was flung into the barrels stacked in the centre of the deck. He scrambled to his feet. Where had Livia gone?

'Livia!' he called. '*Livia!*'

'Over here!' Pale and trembling, she was huddled between two barrels.

The timbers of the ship were creaking and groaning louder and louder as the vessel was pounded by waves.

'I think the ship is breaking up!' Felix shouted in a panic.

He couldn't swim – and neither, he was sure, could Livia. He looked around desperately for something that would float. A few of the jars of garum had already broken, but the barrels stood firm. Would a barrel do? he wondered.

It would have to.

He leaned over to Livia. Her short hair was plastered against her face and her eyes were shut against the salt spray. 'We need to empty a couple of barrels,' he shouted into her ear.

She opened her eyes just wide enough to squint at him. 'What?'

'The barrels – they should float when they're empty.'

He tried to tug the lid off one. It was jammed tight.

'We need something to prise it off with,' Livia gasped.

Felix cast his eyes about the deck for something they could use as a lever. The deck was awash, and it seemed as if everything aboard that wasn't nailed down was being swept along by the surge of water. Amphorae were rolling along the deck like skittles and he saw a single sandal bob past. A fishing net caught around his ankle and he kicked it away. 'There has to be something here we can use!' he said. His attention was caught by a bright blue piece of cloth sailing towards him. Felix recognised it as the sash the captain had been wearing the day he and Livia had boarded the *Tarshish*. It hit Felix's shin with surprising force. The sash was wrapped around something. Picking it up, he unwound the blue fabric to find a long stick. The colour of bone, with intricate carvings, it came up almost to his hip.

Waving the stick, he called to Livia, 'We can use this.'

Livia held first one barrel then another as still as she could while the ship heaved and plunged, and Felix used the stick to wrench off their lids. Together they tipped the barrels, sending pungent fish sauce sloshing across the deck.

'Now what?' Livia gasped.

There was a creak, followed by screams. The ship was breaking in half!

'Get in!' Felix yelled.

Livia swung her legs over the lip of the barrel. Turning to look at Felix, she opened her mouth as if to speak then shook her head and ducked out of sight.

Still clutching the stick, Felix climbed into his own barrel and crouched at the bottom, his head buried in his arms. The deck pitched sharply and suddenly he was rolling, rolling, and for a few brief moments he seemed to be suspended in space before, with a sudden jerk, the barrel hit the sea.

Almost at once he was submerged by a wave, salt water filling his nose and mouth. Coughing and retching, dizzy from bobbing and swirling, he huddled miserably in the barrel, shuddering as it knocked against large pieces of the ship.

His ears were filled with muffled shouts, the roaring wind, and then his barrel collided with something, hard. Thrown forwards by the impact, his head cracked against the side, and everything went black.

Chapter 11

Felix woke with a start. For a few minutes he lay still, almost afraid to open his eyes and see where he was. It occurred to him that he might be lying on the ground beside General Porcius's bed in a tent in Belgica; then he thought perhaps he was in the Underworld.

But the breeze brushing his face was dry and crisp, which seemed unlike either the Underworld or Belgica. He opened his eyes to find he was lying on a small crescent of beach backed by a high cliff. The sun was just peeking above the horizon, washing the pale sand with the watery light of dawn.

I'm alive, he thought, feeling a surge of elation. In the next moment he thought of Livia. If he had survived, surely she had too?

He was half in and half out of his barrel. He crawled free and stood up but immediately fell to his knees, his legs too weak and wobbly to hold him. He lay on the sand for several seconds, gathering his strength, then took a deep breath and tried again.

Upright, leaning on the carved stick for support, he peered up and down the beach. Dotted along the shore were timbers from the deck of the *Tarshish*, a scrap of sail, shards of pottery. There was no sign of another barrel, though. No sign of Livia. No sign of another living soul other than the seagulls circling overhead.

Standing on the deserted beach, he felt overwhelmed by loss and loneliness. He sat on a piece of timber and put his head in his hands.

A seagull squawked. It sounded like it was saying, 'Felix! Felix!'

The seagulls were circling closer now. Irritated, he looked up, raising the stick to shoo them away. As he did, he saw something moving further up the beach.

A figure was running unsteadily along the soft sand.

Livia!

Felix sprang to his feet. 'You're alive!' He was so flooded with joy and relief he felt giddy.

'It was a close call,' she said. 'My barrel broke up on the rocks.' She pointed to the far end of the beach, then gestured to her bloody knees, the cuts on her hands and the scratches on her face.

'I saw the ship going down,' she reported, her voice sombre. 'And the crew with it, I suppose.'

They both stared at the sea in silence. It seemed almost playful this morning, the clear water lapping the shore with a gentle plash. There was no hint of the fearsome power unleashed against the *Tarshish*.

Felix glanced at Livia's face. Her expression, usually so guarded, appeared strangely defenceless. He wondered if she was thinking not just of the ship's crew but of those other people she had lost, like her parents – and perhaps her brother, too.

At last Livia said, 'Let's go.'

'Go where?' Felix asked, lifting his hand to shield his eyes from the glare of the sun.

She gave a weary sigh. 'Rome.'

'Wherever that is,' Felix said wryly.

They walked along the beach towards the rocks where Livia had come ashore. As she pointed out the pieces of her barrel, he realised it was a miracle she had survived.

They clambered over rocks and around a point, and found themselves staring at a beach much like the one they had left behind. Felix was hit by a sense of futility. There could be miles of deserted beaches like this. Hundreds of miles! They might not see another person for—

'Hello there!'

Huh? Felix spun around but he didn't see anyone except Livia, who was looking as bewildered as he felt.

'Up here!'

As he turned to scan the cliff, he saw that perched on top was a villa. And peering over the edge of a terrace was a man.

'There's a path,' the man called, gesturing to their right.

On weak limbs they trudged through the sand to the base of the cliff. Carved into the rock was a set of steep stone steps and they climbed these to the terrace.

They were breathless when they reached the top, and for a few minutes were unable to speak, let alone answer the man's eager questions: 'Where did you two spring from? Who are you? Are you Roman? Have you come to see me?'

Slight, with thinning fair hair, pale eyes and a spotless white tunic, he seemed delighted by their presence. His hands were clasped in front of him and his eyes shone as he regarded them.

'Are we near Rome?' Livia asked.

'Near ... hmm ... well, no. I wouldn't say *near*, exactly.' Then, perhaps noting their crestfallen expressions, he continued, 'I mean, we're not *far*, not as the crow flies. But figuratively speaking ... I mean to say metaphorically ... well, that's the whole trouble, isn't it? I use words too carelessly, you see.'

Felix gaped at him, trying without success to decode what on earth the man was talking about.

'So, we *are* near Rome?' Felix ventured.

'Ah yes, well, so near and yet so far, as they say. I'm afraid there's no way off this island – not for me, at least. I've been banished, don't you know.'

'Banished to an island? Why?' said Livia. Felix felt her astonishment; their host seemed harmless enough. 'Are you a traitor? A criminal?' She shrank away.

'No, no, nothing like that,' the fair-haired man assured her. 'I'm a poet.' He held out his arms and said grandly, 'I am Titus Manius Magius.'

A silence followed, as if the poet was waiting for a reaction.

Felix said, 'Um, hello. I'm Felix and this is my friend Livia.'

'You may know me as Titus,' suggested the poet. 'I wrote some very famous epics. You've probably heard of them.' He glanced at his visitors hopefully.

Felix shook his head. 'Sorry.'

The poet sighed and sank onto a stone couch covered in cushions. 'Oh well. I suppose I'm forgotten in Rome by now.'

'Why were you banished?' Livia asked again.

'I'm afraid I wrote a rather rude poem about, er, Caesar.'

Livia's eyes widened. 'Why did you do that?'

'I thought he would find it amusing … but he didn't. I'm afraid Julius doesn't have much of a sense of humour.' Titus looked around as if to be sure he wouldn't be overheard, then recited:

'*There once was a general called Caesar*
Who suffered a form of amnesia
He said he won all
But he forgot Gaul
What a silly old geezer.'

'Caesar conquered Gaul,' Felix protested.

Titus Magius gave a small smile. 'Not all at once,' he said.

'You mean Gergovia?' From his time in the army Felix knew to never, ever mention what took place in Gergovia. Vercingetorix, a Gallic chieftain, had led a force made up of local tribes in battle against the Romans. Caesar had been forced to order a retreat.

'Anyway, what does Gergovia matter?' Felix continued. 'Caesar won at Alesia and that's what counts. Vercingetorix surrendered and now Gaul belongs to Rome.'

The poet inclined his head. 'As you say. But I was only teasing; I didn't think he'd take it so personally.'

'You called him a silly old geezer and didn't think he'd take it personally?' said Livia.

'With the benefit of hindsight I can see it was a mistake. Look where I've ended up. Oh, the cruelty!'

He gestured to the spacious villa behind them, to the terrace overlooking the sea. The air was fragrant with mimosa. It was the loveliest place Felix had ever seen.

'You should have written a poem that rhymes *Caesar* with *Alesia* instead,' Felix suggested.

'Caesar … Alesia,' Titus repeated. 'Why, you're right. They do rhyme! Let me see …' Drawing himself up, he declaimed:

There once was a general called Caesar
Who won the battle of Alesia …

He nodded thoughtfully. 'What an excellent idea.' Then he slumped. 'It's too late, though.' He sighed.

'I was a favourite of Caesar's once. He loved my epics. If only I could write an epic like I used to. Something that would win me Caesar's favour once again. You'd never know it now, to see the pitiful conditions in which I live, but Julius and I were once great companions. We'd watch the chariot races together, the gladiator contests. And in the evenings I'd amuse him by reading from my latest work. However, I'm a bit short on inspiration these days. Nothing *ever* happens here.'

He crossed his arms and stared out at the sea in a brooding manner. Then he sat up. 'But something *has* happened at last! I have unexpected visitors. If you haven't come looking for me, though, why are you here? Where have you come from?'

'Out there,' said Felix, pointing to the horizon. 'We were on our way to Ostia when there was a terrible storm and our ship was wrecked.'

'We escaped in barrels,' Livia added.

Titus Magius clapped his hands together. 'A shipwreck? Barrels? How exciting! Where had you sailed from?'

'Massilia,' said Livia.

'Before that we'd come from Lutetia,' Felix explained, 'which is where we left the sacred chicken.'

'Felix thinks the chicken cursed us,' Livia said, rolling her eyes.

'What were you doing in Lutetia?' interrupted the poet.

Felix replied, 'Well, the three of us – me, Livia and the sacred chicken – travelled together from Belgica, you see.'

'I don't see at all,' said the poet, his eyes alight with curiosity. 'You'll have to tell me everything.' He held up a hand. 'But where are my manners? You must be hungry after your ordeal and I haven't offered you so much as a grape. Let me see what the servants can rustle up. *Then* you can tell me everything.'

He hurried inside.

'What are we going to do?' Livia whispered. 'We can't tell him the truth.'

'Why not?' Felix asked.

Livia gave him an incredulous look. 'How about because you're an army deserter and I'm a runaway slave and he knows Caesar?'

'So? He can't tell Caesar now, can he? You heard him – he's been banished. Besides, he's very friendly.'

Livia thought about this for a moment, tapping her chin with her index finger. 'I suppose you're right. But you just wait and see how his attitude changes once he finds out what we've done.'

Before Felix could consider what she'd said, Titus Magius returned, followed by two servants carrying platters of dried figs and dates and nuts. 'Just to tide us over till lunchtime.'

He reclined on the couch once more and indicated for Livia and Felix to each take one of the other couches set around a low stone table.

'Now, begin at the beginning.'

Felix glanced at Livia. Whose beginning – his or Livia's?

She gestured to him, and he guessed that she was still feeling reluctant to tell her story.

'It all started in an army camp in Belgica, in the dampest, drizzliest corner of Gaul,' he stated. 'There was a bad omen the day before a battle with the Nervians. Well, several bad omens, actually. I was the servant to General Porcius, a famously unlucky commander who refused to heed the signs. The worst of it was when the sacred chickens refused their grain but General Porcius declared his intention to fight anyway.'

'Oh, that's bad,' said Titus. 'Didn't he remember what happened to Publius Claudius Pulcher?'

'He didn't care,' Felix said. 'But I didn't want to become a Nervian slave, so I ran away from camp that night.'

He was reminded again that his story and Livia's weren't that different: they were both running away from being slaves. Still, to speak it aloud like that made him realise the enormity of his decision that day: to desert from the army was a shameful, cowardly act. Livia was right; now that Titus Magius knew the truth about Felix he would surely condemn him. Felix hung his head.

The poet sucked a particularly persistent piece of date from between his teeth then said in a matter-of-fact way: 'Of course you ran away. One should never ignore an omen like that. You were sensible to leave.'

And so, emboldened, Felix unfolded their tale. The poet gasped at Livia's capture, cheered at Felix's daring theft of the chariot and, when Felix recounted the sad fate of the crew of the *Tarshish*, wiped away tears.

'Have you ever thought of becoming a poet?' he asked when Felix was done.

'Me?' said Felix, surprised. 'A poet?'

'Why not? You certainly know how to tell a story. What an adventure! It would make a wonderful epic poem. Wait!' He rose, put a hand to his brow and stood gazing out to sea for several minutes. Then he turned to face them and, holding out his arms, began to declaim:

'A serpent of enormous size,
A flash of lightning breaks the skies;

Ill omens for the army of Rome—
Our hero decides to flee for home.'

'Wow – that's great!' said Felix.

'Yes,' said Livia, 'it sounds very promising. But how soon can we leave?'

The poet was taken aback by her impatience. 'Leave? But you only just got here. Please stay awhile. It's been so long since I had company.'

'We need to get to Rome before the gladiator games to celebrate Caesar's triumph,' Felix reminded him. 'Because of Livia's brother.'

The poet looked ashamed. 'Of course, how selfish of me.' He screwed up his face in thought. 'As I said, I am forbidden to leave the island, but that doesn't mean you are. If you go down to the harbour, someone there should be able to signal to a passing ship for you. Let us have lunch, then we'll see if I can equip you a little better for your journey.'

On the poet's orders, the servants took Felix and Livia inside and tended to their cuts and grazes. They took it in turns to bathe, and were each given one of the poet's own tunics of fine soft cotton.

'Much better,' said Titus when they presented themselves to him. His eyes went to the stick Felix still carried. 'Is that the stick you used to open the barrels?'

Felix nodded. 'It belonged to the captain.' Abruptly, he had a vision of the scene he'd witnessed the night before the *Tarshish* sailed. 'Though he got it from a Roman general.'

'May I see?'

Felix handed the stick to him and Titus turned it in his hand, peering at the carvings. 'Hmm, it looks like ivory,' he said. 'It might even be a sceptre.'

Felix looked at the stick with surprise. 'You mean it could have belonged to a king?'

'Perhaps,' said the poet. 'But since the captain is drowned, and you are unlikely to encounter the general again, we'll probably never know.' He returned the stick to Felix and said, 'Now, let's have lunch.'

That afternoon, after a lunch of fish smothered in a rich cheesy sauce, they set off down the road to the harbour dressed in their new tunics and old cloaks, with Felix carrying the stick and Livia carrying a satchel containing a loaf of bread, some hard cheese and a waterskin, as well as a small pouch of coins to pay for their passage to Ostia.

'Think of it as a thankyou gift,' Titus had said as he gave them the pouch. 'I am going to turn your tale into the most thrilling epic Rome has ever known. If I ever get home it will make my reputation.'

As Felix and Livia walked, they mused on the reason for the poet's kindness.

'We told him the truth yet he didn't treat us differently,' Felix noted. 'In fact, he helped us. He must have a very kind heart.'

Livia looked thoughtful. 'I think it's more than that,' she said. 'I think he reacted the way he did because of how well you told our story. The way you described what we were thinking and feeling meant he had to think of us as more than just a slave and a deserter. I suppose that's what makes a good storyteller: the ability to make listeners understand why people act as they do and empathise with them.'

Felix had never realised it before, but he saw now that poets could be very powerful.

They reached the small fishing port not long after. There, in exchange for one of their coins, the harbourmaster agreed to signal a ship for them. 'Though you could be waiting a while,' he warned. 'We're a bit out of the way here.'

In the end, it was dusk before a passing ship responded to the signal. The harbourmaster rowed them out and hailed the captain.

'I have two young people here seeking passage to Ostia,' he called.

'We've just come from there,' came the reply. 'We delivered a load of grain and now we're on our way back to Alexandria.'

Felix and Livia looked at each other in dismay. 'That's in Egypt, isn't it?' Livia asked.

Felix nodded. 'It's the home of Cleopatra.'

'Is it very far?'

They were so close to Rome he could almost smell the sewers. 'I think it takes about two weeks to sail from Alexandria to Ostia.'

'Well?' said the harbourmaster. 'Are you going aboard? I would if I were you. I don't know when the next ship will be along and you'll easily find passage back to Rome from Alexandria.'

Livia considered for a moment then sighed. 'I suppose we should. At least we'll be moving – even if it's in the wrong direction. We could still reach Rome by the beginning of April.'

The grain ship was much larger than the *Tarshish* and, thanks to the generosity of Titus Magius, Felix and Livia had a cabin to themselves. There were several other passengers, including merchants, some dignitaries and even a few military men, but they found the sailors were much more interesting company. One in particular, Amoses – an Egyptian with dark chin-length hair and wide-set brown eyes – became a good friend.

One afternoon about midway through their journey, while Felix and Livia sat with him as he mended a sail, Amoses told them about Alexandria, the capital of Egypt, and its ruler, the queen Cleopatra. 'She might be young, but she's smart,' he said. 'She originally inherited the throne with her brother, Ptolemy XIII, then he seized power for himself. Almost caused a war, so Julius Caesar came from Rome to Alexandria to put a stop to it. Didn't want the supply of grain to Rome to be interrupted, you see. Cleopatra went to Julius Caesar to seek his support. And how do you think she managed to get into the palace where he was staying without one of her enemies trying to stop her?' He tapped the side of his nose. 'I'll tell you how: she rolled herself up in a carpet and had it delivered to Caesar.'

Livia nodded approvingly. 'She does sound clever.'

The sailor pulled the needle through the sail and gave it a tug. 'Now Cleopatra's on the throne, but really it's Rome who rules Egypt ... and that's the sail fixed.' He knotted the thread then leaned over to bite off the end with his teeth.

Felix's eye was caught by a silver amulet dangling from a leather cord around the man's neck. 'The shape of your pendant – is that like some kind of sailor's knot?' he asked.

The sailor glanced down at his chest. 'Oh no – this is the buckle of the girdle of Isis.'

'She's the protector of sailors, isn't she?' asked Livia. 'I think I've heard some of the crew asking for her blessing.'

'That's right: Isis protects sailors and merchants. She's another clever one: when her husband Osiris was murdered by his brother Set, she assumed the form of a bird – a black kite – and searched all Egypt for his body. She then fanned him back to life with her wings.'

And so the fortnight passed in stories and sailors' lore, until early one afternoon there came a cry from the crow's nest: the lighthouse of Alexandria was in sight.

Chapter 12

Felix's first view of Alexandria was of a harbour busy with ships large and small, and docks crowded with sailors and cargo.

'What is that?' he yelped, pointing to a crate that held a creature as low to the ground as a serpent but with enormous jaws and an enormous number of glistening teeth.

Livia was the one to supply him with an answer. 'It's a crocodile,' she said. 'Roman ladies put the dung on their faces; they think it makes their skin pale.'

'They actually put the poo on their faces?' Felix said in disbelief. He laughed – but Livia didn't join in.

'Crocodiles are also used in the arena ... to kill condemned prisoners.' She shuddered and Felix knew that she must be thinking of her brother, perhaps wondering if this very crocodile might be part of the spectacle Caesar had planned.

'As soon as we disembark we'll start looking for passage to Rome,' he promised as their ship nudged up against the quay.

Half an hour later they were on dry land, feeling unsteady on their legs after a fortnight at sea.

'I think I need to sit down for a few minutes,' Livia confessed. 'Or I might fall down.'

They bought some bread and snacks from a stall on the quay and went to sit in a shady square by the port.

As soon as Felix tore a hunk of bread from the loaf, a bird with wings like fingers glided from the cloudless sky to settle on a nearby branch.

It gave a piercing cry.

'I think it must be a kite,' Felix said. 'Like the one Amoses was telling us about. They're probably considered sacred here.'

Livia groaned. 'Don't talk to me about sacred birds. One was enough.' She addressed the bird: 'You're not a sacred kite, are you? Please tell me you're not.'

The bird just regarded them steadily.

'I think it's hungry,' Felix said.

'There's something it has in common with your chicken then.'

'It wasn't *my* chicken,' Felix objected. He glanced down at the ring he still wore on his thumb. 'You can't *own* a sacred chicken. It's a privilege if they elect to help you.' He held out a piece of sausage and the bird swooped down to take it.

As he bit into a pepper stuffed with spicy lentils, he watched what was going on around him. Alexandria! It felt astonishing to be here in the city that had been founded by Alexander the Great. Gazing past the warehouses and taverns that lined the quay, he had a glimpse of red-tiled roofs that hinted at grand buildings in the city beyond the port. It was a pity they wouldn't have time to explore ...

He turned his attention back to the harbour. They would need to find a ship bound for Rome as soon as possible – preferably one that didn't include crocodiles among its cargo.

Almost immediately his eyes landed on a Roman galley – a naval vessel, judging by the flag fluttering from its mast. As Felix watched, a commander in full uniform descended the gangway to the quay, where a young woman who had just alighted from a barge stood waiting, a basket by her feet. She wore a long pleated dress of white linen, wide gold bracelets on each arm and long gold earrings. A beaded headdress encircled her jet-black hair.

He wasn't the only one watching the pair exchange formal greetings, he realised, as he caught sight of two shifty-looking men who were slowly but surely edging nearer.

'Why do I always have to share my food with birds?' Livia said, sighing.

Felix turned to see that she was holding out a piece of sausage for the kite. He smiled to himself. She pretended to be so hard, but really she had a soft heart.

He glanced back to the quay just in time to see one of the shifty-looking men dart over and snatch the young woman's basket.

'Hey!' he yelled.

The Egyptian and the Roman were still exchanging greetings; neither had noticed the swift movement of the shifty man.

As the thief and his companion sprinted down a narrow street between two warehouses, Felix leaped up and ran after them.

The narrow street turned into another, and then another, becoming a maze of alleyways, some lined with workshops and others showing nothing but high blank walls to the street.

Felix pursued the men, the alleyways growing increasingly deserted, increasingly dark, until he was navigating by the sound of running footsteps – and then the footsteps ceased and all was quiet. He'd lost them.

He looked around, trying to find some landmark among the blank stone walls. Had he turned left into this alley, or right? He started to walk slowly, attempting to retrace his steps, when a hand closed around his throat and pressed him up against the wall.

'What do we have here then?' It was one of the thieves. His face was so close that Felix could smell the garlic on his breath.

'I think it must be a Roman spy,' a voice hissed. The second thief – younger than the first, Felix saw – stepped forwards to join them.

The older thief frowned and loosened his grip on Felix, who drew a ragged breath. 'Aren't the Romans our allies?' His brow was furrowed. 'Julius Caesar won the Battle of the Nile and put Cleopatra on the throne.'

'Hmm, I don't know,' said the young thief. 'Let's take him somewhere a bit more private and question him.'

'Good idea.' The older thief grasped Felix's arm and began to drag him down the alleyway. But as they left the seclusion of the shadows the older thief gasped. 'He's got red hair!' He released Felix as though he'd been burned.

Felix stiffened. *Uh-oh.* Was it some kind of curse here to have red hair?

'What good luck!' said the younger man. 'Rameses II, the great pharaoh, had red hair too.'

Felix felt limp with relief. *Phew!*

'No, no,' the older man insisted. 'Red hair is unlucky.' He gnawed on his knuckle worriedly, staring at Felix's hair with an expression of horror. 'The sensible thing would be to bury him alive.'

Uh-oh …

'Though the god Set has red hair *and* he's the protector of foreigners,' the younger thief argued. 'We should let the boy go.'

Phew!

The older man shook his head, unconvinced. 'Set is also the god of chaos and disorder and storms,' he countered. 'And—' he stabbed his finger at Felix emphatically '—Set murdered his brother Osiris.'

Uh-oh …

Felix glanced at the younger thief hopefully, but he was nodding his agreement.

'You're right,' he said. He shot Felix a look of distaste. 'So what should we do with him?'

The older thief thought for a moment. 'I know — let's sacrifice him to Osiris.'

The younger man's eyes lit up. 'Yes! Then we can burn his body and scatter the ashes in a field to ensure a fertile harvest.'

UH-OH!

The older man waved a dismissive hand. 'Don't be absurd. We're hardly going to do that.'

Phew! Felix sagged against the wall.

'We don't have the time,' the older thief concluded. 'We'll just slit his throat and leave him.' His hand moved down to a knife tucked in his belt. 'Take him back to the alley,' he directed, 'and I'll do it there.'

'No!' Felix tried to run but the younger man snatched his arm and squeezed it in a grip so tight Felix cried out.

'Oh no, you don't.' Hooking his arm around Felix's neck in a chokehold, he dragged him back into the shadows.

As the older man drew the knife from his belt, Felix began to tremble. And to think he'd called General Porcius unlucky!

Felix let out a whimper as the young man wrenched his head back to expose Felix's throat. As the cold blade of the knife touched his flesh, he closed his eyes. When he next opened them, he would be in the Underworld.

Chapter 13

'My sons ...'

At the sound of the rasping voice, Felix opened his eyes. The knife that had been pressed against his throat was hastily concealed.

Silhouetted in the entrance to the alley was the bent figure of an old woman.

'What are you doing, my sons?'

Leaning heavily on her walking stick, she took two tottering steps towards them.

'Wh-who are you?' the younger thief asked.

'I am a priestess of Isis,' she intoned. 'And she has bid me come here. But why?' She thrust her head forwards as if squinting. 'Why am I here?'

'W-we don't know, mistress,' said the older thief.

'Then I must wait for a sign,' the priestess rasped.

She half raised a trembling hand and then tapped her shoulder twice.

For a moment nothing happened. Then there came a harsh cry from above, drawing their attention upwards. A dark shape swooped from the sky and came to rest on the old woman's hunched shoulder.

The thieves took a step back so that they were behind Felix.

'Is that a kite on her shoulder?' one whispered.

'It must be a sacred kite of Isis,' muttered the other.

The priestess was still peering at them. 'My sons, is this boy your prisoner?'

'H-he is a thief.' The older man gestured to the basket on the ground.

As Felix opened his mouth to protest, the other added, 'And a foreigner. With *red hair*.'

'Ah,' said the woman, nodding. 'I see. So, the boy is a son of Set. You did well to capture him, my sons.' She paused, then cocked her head. 'What is that?'

'I didn't say any—'

'Not you,' she rasped, hushing the thief. 'Tell me, o sacred bird, what is your will?'

Felix's heart began to pound as the bird fixed its beady gaze on him. Was he about to be sacrificed to Osiris after all?

Abruptly the bird launched itself from the old priestess's shoulder and flew towards the trio. It circled them twice before coming to rest on Felix's left shoulder.

Its claws dug into his skin and Felix was only able to resist crying out for fear of alarming the bird and causing it to tighten its grip still further.

The priestess nodded. 'Yes, I see,' she murmured. Then, raising her voice, she said, 'You must release this son of Set. Osiris and Isis forgive him.'

The two thieves gazed at her open-mouthed.

'Go, son of Set!' She thrust out her hand dramatically, pointing to the entrance of the alleyway.

The bird took off and Felix, almost stumbling in his haste, followed it.

He had no idea where he was; he had become hopelessly lost while chasing the thieves. But the bird was ahead of him – had saved him – so he kept following it through the tangle of streets, none of which seemed familiar.

After what seemed like an eternity, they reached a square and the bird flew up to rest on the branch of a tree. Gazing around him, Felix felt a moment of joy as he recognised the square he had been sitting in. But, he saw, his heart sinking, there was no sign of his friend.

'Why do you have to walk so fast?' a rasping voice behind him scolded. 'How do you expect an old woman to keep up?'

Turning, Felix saw the priestess. She was leaning on her stick and holding the basket the thieves had stolen.

'I believe this is yours?'

'No,' said Felix. 'It belonged to a woman who was here earlier.' He gestured towards the quay where the Roman commander and Egyptian woman had been conversing. Though the ship and barge remained, there was no sign of the pair. 'Those other men stole it, not me.'

'Do you really expect me to believe that?'

The old woman straightened and threw back the hood on her cloak.

'*Livia!*' said Felix. For several seconds he just gaped at her, too astonished to speak. When his voice returned, he said, 'That was you in the alley? *You* were the priestess?'

'Me and my sacred bird,' his friend agreed.

Felix shook his head in wonder. 'You were amazing. But how did you manage to plan all that?'

Livia laughed. 'I didn't plan any of it! I just ran after you when you chased the thieves. I brought your stick in case I needed to hit someone.' She held out the stick. 'I started to get really worried when I heard them talking about making sacrifices, then I remembered the story Amoses told us about Isis and the kite.'

Felix looked at the bird preening its feathers on the branch above them. 'But what was the kite doing there? How did you get it to obey your orders?'

Livia shrugged. 'When I took off it flew after me. Wanted more of this, I suppose.' She opened her palm to reveal the end of a sausage, which she flung onto the ground.

In a lightning-quick move, the bird swooped down and tore at it with its beak.

'When it saw you in the alley it must have recognised you from when you fed it earlier,' Livia speculated. 'Meantime, I wonder what happened to the girl who lost this?' She gestured to the basket she still carried. 'We should try to return it.'

Felix surveyed their surrounds anxiously. The light was fading, the shadows growing long. The port was likely to be a dangerous place after dark. 'We need to find passage on a ship as soon as possible,' he said, scanning the docks.

'It's almost dusk; there'll be no more ships sailing tonight,' Livia pointed out.

'Well, we can't hang around here. Let's find an inn where we can spend the night. Then we can come back at dawn and ask around for passage.'

'I think there was a main street just a couple of blocks inland from the harbour,' Livia said, pointing. 'We crossed it when we were chasing the thieves.'

Felix took the satchel and Livia carried the basket, and they set off back along the narrow street the thieves had taken, emerging onto a wide boulevard.

Keen to put some distance between them and the raffish port, they walked quickly at first, passing baths and temples, grand houses and shops with barely a glance. But as the sandy spaces between the buildings grew larger, and the buildings themselves grew smaller and shabbier, Felix realised they must be nearing the edge of town.

He stopped a man hurrying past with a scroll held tightly in one hand. 'Excuse me, do you know of an inn nearby?'

The man paused and tapped his lip thoughtfully. 'There's a caravanserai just beyond the city limits.' He gestured over his shoulder, where the buildings petered out.

Felix peered in the direction the man was pointing. All he could see was sand.

'What's a carasa— a canavar—' Felix gave up.

'A caravanserai,' the man repeated patiently. 'It's like an inn, but larger. It's for travellers who have come from the desert.'

Felix glanced at Livia, who shrugged.

'That'll do,' she said.

'Keep going that way,' said the man. 'You can't miss it.'

The caravanserai was further away than it seemed, though, and it was dark by the time they reached an imposing gate with a lantern hung beside the entrance.

'Hello?' Felix called.

The innkeeper stepped out to meet them.

'We're looking for a room for the night,' Felix said.

The innkeeper looked from Felix to Livia, then craned his neck to peer over their shoulders into the dark. 'Who are you travelling with? Where's your camel?'

'Our, uh, camel is hurt,' Felix invented. 'And our father stayed with it. He sent us ahead to, uh ...'

Turning towards Livia, he widened his eyes and shrugged almost imperceptibly.

'To buy some camel ointment from the ...' Livia trailed off, the silence stretching so long that both Felix and the innkeeper seemed to lean into it. 'From the camel ointment market,' she finished.

The innkeeper rocked back on his heels. 'The camel ointment market?' he repeated. 'What camel ointment market? I've never heard of such a thing.'

Livia affected surprise. 'I thought surely a city as big and important as Alexandria would have a market specialising in camel ointments and liniments and so forth,' she said. 'In Rome we have three.'

Before the innkeeper could question this further – he might ask, for example, why Rome had three markets devoted to camel ointments but no actual camels – Felix pulled Titus's purse from the satchel.

At the sight of it the innkeeper's expression smoothed and he said, 'I believe we have a room on the upper level, if that would suit you.'

'Thank you,' said Felix. 'It would.'

The innkeeper showed them to a bare room with two narrow cots, then stumped back down the stairs.

Felix stretched out on one of the cots and immediately sat back up. 'I'm hungry. Do we have anything left to eat?'

Livia shook her head as she sat down on the cot opposite. 'I gave the last of it to the bird.'

Felix lay down again. 'We should have asked the innkeeper if he served food.'

Livia shook her head again. 'I'm not going back down there. What if he asks about the ointment markets?'

Felix gave a snort of laughter. 'What were you thinking? *In Rome we have three.*'

Livia giggled. 'I panicked,' she said. 'Anyway, let me check the basket – maybe the Egyptian woman was delivering food to the Roman galley.'

'It might be cake,' said Felix, thinking of the sacred chicken.

Livia pulled back the cloth covering the basket. 'No, there's nothing to eat. There's only this.' She took out a package wrapped in linen so fine it was almost transparent.

Felix got up from his cot and joined Livia on hers, watching as she unwrapped the linen to reveal a small wooden box inlaid with mother of pearl. Slowly she lifted the lid.

'What is it?' Felix asked, trying to peer over the lid of the box.

'Coins,' Livia breathed. 'Gold coins.' She counted. 'Twelve of them.'

She held out a gleaming coin and Felix took one.

'This side has a picture of Caesar,' he said, studying it. Flipping it over, he saw the profile of a woman with dead-straight hair and a dead-straight nose. 'I bet this is Cleopatra,' he said.

'They look really valuable,' Livia said. 'We have to return them.'

'Tomorrow,' said Felix, smothering a yawn. 'We'll find the woman we saw by the quay and give them back to her.' He stood up and went back to his own cot. 'I really wish she had been carrying food though.'

Chapter 14

Felix woke early, roused by hunger pangs.

He glanced over at Livia and saw that she was still sleeping. She seemed so peaceful he hated to disturb her – but he had to eat. Taking the waterskin and a few coins from the purse Titus had given them, he left the room to see if he could buy some food and fill their flask.

The stairs outside their room led to a central paved courtyard in which stood dozens of camels and mules. Felix quickly spotted a boy carrying a tray of flatbreads, and he exchanged a coin for two rounds of bread. Biting into one, he surveyed the traders in long robes loading up their animals. 'Where are they going?' he asked the boy who'd sold him the bread.

The boy shrugged. 'Some are taking goods to sell at the markets here in Alexandria. Some are going the other way, across the desert.'

Felix walked further into the courtyard, heading towards the well in the centre. As he weaved around the camels and their masters, he couldn't help staring. He'd never seen a camel up close. In fact, he'd never seen one from a distance either. He was surprised to learn they were tall – taller even than General Porcius's stallion – with large humps on their backs, skinny legs, long necks and long noses. Their thick coats were the colour of the desert sand he could see through the open gate of the caravanserai.

Most of the camels ignored him as he slipped between them, but one who was standing off to the side gave Felix a curious look as he passed.

Pausing, Felix broke off a piece of bread and held it out.

The camel extended its long neck to take the bread from Felix's palm with its big lips.

Tentatively, Felix reached out to pat the camel's furry snout. 'Hello, camel,' he said. 'My name's Felix.'

The camel paused in its chewing, blinked its long lashes and said, 'My name is Felix too!'

'Really?' said Felix. 'That's funny.' He took another bite of bread and tore off a second piece for Felix the camel.

'Where are you going? My friend and I are going to Rome.'

Through a mouthful of bread the camel replied, 'We're going to Rome too!'

Felix regarded the camel with surprise. 'I thought you could only get to Rome from here by ship,' he said.

'I'm a ship too!' the camel said brightly.

Felix supposed he was right; he did recall hearing camels spoken of as ships of the desert. 'Well, maybe I'll see you in Rome then.'

He continued on to the well, filled the waterskin, then headed back to the room and Livia. He should probably wake her, he thought, as they would need to find the Egyptian woman to return the coins before finding passage on a ship to Rome.

The activity in the courtyard seemed to have increased while Felix had his back turned. It was as if some signal had been given, and people were moving at double speed.

'Why is everyone in such a hurry?' he asked the innkeeper, who was standing at the bottom of the stairs with his hands on his hips, watching the bustle.

'We've just heard that a patrol of Roman soldiers is on its way. They're searching for two thieves, apparently. No one wants their journey delayed while the soldiers question them.'

At once Felix thought of the two men he'd encountered the day before. 'I think I might have seen the thieves down at the port,' he volunteered.

The innkeeper raised his eyebrows. 'Is that so? They're saying two young Romans were seen at the port yesterday – and they stole some precious coins. *Very* precious …'

He must be referring to the gold coins he and Livia had found in the basket, Felix realised.

'The thieves I saw were local men,' he began.

But the innkeeper shook his head. 'No, they definitely weren't locals. Two young travellers arrived yesterday on a ship from Rome, they reckon, just before the coins were stolen.' He shook his head. 'I wouldn't like to be in their shoes when they're caught. They'll have quite a punishment in store, I bet.'

'Wh-what kind of punishment?' Felix quavered.

'My guess is they'll be buried alive in a tomb,' said the innkeeper with relish. Then, as if realising who he was talking to, he said, 'Hold on … didn't your sister say something about Rome yesterday?'

'N-no, I don't think so,' Felix said.

'Yes, she did – she was talking about the markets of Rome.' The innkeeper's eyes narrowed.

'Oh, that,' said Felix, with a nervous laugh. 'You might have thought she said "Rome" but she was probably saying "home". She often says "r" in the place of "h". You know ... calls for *relp* when she's in trouble and, uh, prefers to bathe in *rot* water.'

The innkeeper was staring at him with a look that mingled suspicion and incredulity.

'I'd better be going,' Felix babbled. 'Our father will be waiting ... with the camel ...' He spun around and took the stairs two at a time.

Bursting into the room, he called, 'Livia. *Livia!* Wake up!'

She sat up abruptly. 'What is it?' She rubbed her eyes. 'Why did you let me sleep so long? We need to get back to the port to find a ship. Oh, and return those coins ...'

'We're going to have to change our plans,' Felix said urgently. 'Listen.' Quickly, he repeated what the innkeeper had said about the stolen coins.

'You mean they think *we're* the thieves? Well, we'll just tell them the truth. It was those two men.'

'We have no proof,' Felix pointed out. 'And we *do* have the basket with the coins. Do you think the patrol will believe us?'

Livia's face fell. 'Probably not,' she admitted. She stared at Felix, her expression desperate. 'What are we going to do?' she said. 'I have to get to Rome. My brother …' She paused, then continued: 'But we can't risk being seen hanging around by the docks. If only there were ships leaving from somewhere else.'

I'm a ship too … Felix was struck by an idea. 'I think there *is* another way to Rome,' he said. 'There's a camel caravan downstairs about to leave for Rome. Maybe we can travel with them.'

They hastily gathered their belongings. Felix put the remaining flatbread and waterskin into the satchel and picked it up. Grasping his stick, he said, 'Ready?'

Livia was holding the basket, looking uncertain. 'What should we do with the coins? Maybe we should leave them here.'

'But if they find them in our room, then they'll take it as proof we stole them in the first place and they might come after us,' Felix pointed out.

'I don't know,' said Livia doubtfully. 'Taking them seems wrong.'

They stared at each other in indecision, then Felix said, 'If we don't leave now the camel train might leave without us. Let's take the coins and then, when we've put some distance between us and Alexandria, give them to someone who's travelling in this direction.' He handed the satchel to Livia, who shoved the box inside then slung the satchel over her shoulder. She kicked the basket under the cot, where it wouldn't be seen.

'Oh, and Livia,' said Felix as they left the room, 'when you see the innkeeper, say "rello".'

Livia gaped at him. 'What? Why would I do that?'

'I don't have time to explain – but it's important.'

Livia was unconvinced, yet as they passed the innkeeper at the foot of the stairs she called out, 'Rello! Rello!'

'Uh, yes ... hello,' the innkeeper responded, giving Felix a nod of understanding.

'Phew,' Felix said under his breath. 'It worked.'

Leading the way across the courtyard, he told Livia, 'Get this: one of the camels is also named Felix.'

Livia eyed him sideways. 'Do you know this for a fact, or are you presuming it because you look so much alike?'

'He told me.'

'What, the *camel* told you? In words?'

'That's right – he spoke to me.'

Livia heaved a deep sigh. 'Here we go again. It's not a sacred camel, is it?'

Felix frowned. 'I don't think so.'

They reached the place where Felix (the boy) had encountered Felix (the camel) to find half-a-dozen camels kneeling in a line, each with a pair of saddlebags draped across its hump.

'Excuse me?' Felix called.

A tall, thin man in long sand-coloured robes raised his head from the saddlebag he was tightening. 'Yes?'

'Is this your camel train?'

The man inclined his head. 'It is. I am Merybad. Perfumes and incense; frankincense and myrrh.'

'We'd like to travel with you,' Felix said.

The trader stroked his short, silky black beard. 'I don't usually take passengers.'

'We can pay.' Felix nudged Livia, who pulled the coin purse Titus had given them from her satchel. She upended it on her palm. Only three coins left.

The trader was shaking his head. 'I'm sorry, but for such a long journey ... And I presume I will have to share my supplies with you?'

In the distance, Felix heard a rhythmic stamping, familiar from his time in the army. The patrol was drawing near. 'One of the other coins, Livia,' he whispered urgently.

She gave him a searching look. 'Are you sure?'

He gave a single, quick nod and Livia thrust her hand into her satchel, rummaged, then produced one of the gold coins.

She held it out to the trader.

Merybad picked it up, examined one side, raised his eyebrows slightly, and then flipped the coin over to examine the other side.

'As I said, I don't usually take passengers – but in this case I'd be happy to make an exception.' He slipped the gold coin into a pocket in his robe. 'I'm leaving straightaway, though.'

'The sooner the better,' said Felix.

'Very well. You may ride the camel on the end.'

'It's Felix,' said Felix to Livia as they hurried towards the last of the kneeling camels.

Felix the camel blinked his long lashes and gave a rubbery-lipped smile.

When Felix and Livia were balanced on the camel's hump, the trader uttered a word that sounded like '*shah*' and, as one, the camels rose to their feet, stamping and huffing.

With a jingling of harnesses and a swaying of saddlebags, the camel train filed out of the courtyard.

Felix, riding Felix, risked a glance over his shoulder as they lumbered up the sandy street that ended in desert sands, just in time to see the Roman patrol reach the entrance to the caravanserai.

'You have to admit, this isn't a bad way to travel,' Felix said to Livia as he searched in the satchel then handed her the flatbread he'd bought for her and chewed on the remains of his own.

'Not too bad at all,' she agreed.

But as the hours passed, Felix found his enjoyment waning as the landscape never changed. Sand to the left and sand to the right. Sand ahead and sand behind. The vast plains of sand were occasionally punctuated by huge rocky crags. Sometimes they would navigate narrow valleys between the crags. On occasion they would even climb sand dunes, which at first revived Felix's interest. He couldn't wait to see the view from the top. Were there many big cities between Alexandria and Rome? he wondered.

But at the top they just saw more sand.

And so it continued, day after day, plodding on and on across the sandy expanse between outcrops of rock from dawn to dusk. When night fell, they shared a simple meal provided by Merybad. One of the half-dozen camels carried the supplies: huge goatskin water sacks and bags of grain. The trader mixed the grain and water together then baked the dough in the coals of a fire to make a type of bread. The meals were quiet affairs. Merybad was proving to be a man of few words, unlike his camel Felix, who grew more talkative each day. Felix (the boy) had made the mistake of remarking on the never-ending vista of sand, and the camel had been quick to agree, a torrent of words streaming from him as he narrated every step of the journey.

'I can see sand too!

'I can see more sand!

'I can see lots of sandy sand!'

Livia gritted her teeth and muttered, 'He's even more annoying than the chicken.'

'He means well, though,' Felix defended his namesake.

The nights were sharp and cold in the desert. Merybad arranged the camels in a circle and they slept on rugs in their midst, cloaks wrapped tight around them.

On the fifth morning, as they bundled up their cloaks and prepared to take their places aboard Felix the camel, Livia gazed out across the sand, and more sand, and lots of sandy sand, and said in a weary tone, 'How many days is it till we reach Rome? I don't know how much more of that camel's voice I can bear.'

Felix shrugged. He hadn't thought to ask how long it would take a ship of the desert to reach Rome; he'd just presumed it would take the same amount of time as a ship of the sea. 'I'm not sure. I'll ask Merybad.'

He approached the trader, who was bent over a kneeling camel, rearranging its load.

'Excuse me, Merybad,' Felix said. 'Is it much further to Rome?'

The trader straightened and turned to stare at him. 'Rome?' He looked astonished. 'We're not going to Rome – we're going to Babylon.'

'*What?*' Felix's heart plummeted. 'Babylon?'

'That's right. We'll carry on across the desert till we reach the Euphrates river, then we'll follow it to Babylon. We should be there in two months, maybe three.'

'Babylon?' Felix repeated, his voice rising in panic. 'Three months? I don't understand. You're supposed to be going to Rome!'

The trader's brow creased. 'Who told you we were going to Rome?'

'Felix did!'

The crease grew deeper. 'I thought *you* were Felix.'

'I mean Felix the camel. The one we're riding.' Felix pointed to the last camel of the train.

'Him? Who told you his name was Felix? He hasn't got a name. He's just a camel.'

This was news to Felix (the boy). 'But if he doesn't have a name, how do you call him?'

'I usually say, "Hey, you with the hump." Or sometimes I call him Big Nose.'

'I see.' Felix stood frozen to the spot, trying to take this all in.

The trader watched him curiously. 'Was there anything else?'

'Uh, no. Well, I'd better go tell Livia about Babylon.'

With a heavy feeling in his chest, Felix returned to Livia and the camel (not Felix).

'What's wrong, Felix?' asked Livia, reading his mood.

'My name is Felix!' chimed in the camel.

'No, it's not!' said Felix (the boy). 'I was speaking to Merybad, and he said your name *isn't* Felix.'

'My name isn't Felix!' said the camel agreeably.

'He said he calls you Big Nose,' Felix persisted.

'My name's Big Nose!'

'And that we're not going to Rome – we're going to Babylon.' He delivered this last sentence as an accusation.

'We're going to Babylon!' the camel agreed.

'Wait,' Livia interrupted. 'We're going to Babylon? What do you mean, *we're going to Babylon?*'

'Merybad just told me.' Felix swallowed. 'It's going to take three months.'

'Three months! But I don't even know where Babylon is,' said Livia in despair, 'and it must be the Ides of March already. I need to be in Rome within the next month!'

'I'm sorry,' said Felix, hanging his head. 'I probably should have asked more questions before we left Alexandria. But Felix – I mean Big Nose – said ...'

'Why did you listen to such a silly camel?' Livia snapped.

'He's not that bad,' Felix protested. 'He can talk.'

'That's not a bonus,' said Livia. Even though her words were harsh, Felix could hear the quiver in her voice and see the glimmer of tears in her eyes.

They'd fled Belgica two months ago, and instead of getting closer to Rome they were further away than ever. And Felix was to blame.

'I'm sorry, Livia,' he repeated. 'I'll find a way to fix this, I promise. Let me talk to Merybad again.'

As he trudged back across the sand to the head of the camel train, he ran through the options. Though as far as he could tell, there was only one option: that they return to Alexandria – which meant losing another five days — where they would have to evade the patrols that were no doubt still looking for them, and find a ship bound for Rome, preferably with a captain who wouldn't ask too many questions.

Merybad, now busy with the lead camel's harness, looked up as Felix approached.

'You have explained the situation to your friend?'

'Yes,' said Felix. 'But we need to be in Rome by the middle of April, so I think we're going to have to turn back. Thank you for bringing us this far. I'm sorry for the misunderstanding.'

Merybad's expression grew troubled. 'If I could spare the time I'd take you to Alexandria myself, however I have urgent business in Babylon. And I really wouldn't recommend you attempt the journey on your own; you'll never find your way through the desert.' He waved at the featureless expanse around them, and Felix's heart plunged even further. The trader was right.

'Could we buy a camel?' Felix suggested. He was thinking of the gold coins. They'd used one already and he was reluctant to use another, but this was an emergency. 'They seem to know the route pretty well.'

The trader shook his head. 'I regret that won't be possible.'

'Then tell me,' Felix begged, 'if you were in my position, what would you do?'

Merybad stroked his beard for a moment then, gesturing for Felix to join him, he squatted on the ground. With his finger, he sketched a map in the sand.

'In a week or so we'll reach an oasis city called Tadmor, where you will be able to find transport to one of the ports on the coast – Tripoli would be the closest. From there you can sail to Ostia in three weeks.'

Felix stared at the map, trying to gauge the distance from Tadmor to the coast. A few days, perhaps? That meant at least five more weeks of travel, he calculated. Would they make it to Rome in time? He sighed and stood up. It was starting to look like they wouldn't, he realised, with a tight feeling in his throat.

Still, for Livia's sake – and her brother's – they would have to try.

Chapter 15

Late that afternoon, they reached a caravanserai. Here they would stop for the night and Merybad would exchange news with the other merchants and travellers.

The caravanserai was larger than the one in Alexandria, perhaps because it was the only one for miles and miles. As they entered the courtyard Felix was surprised to see so many other travellers. About fifty camels knelt on the flagstones, and dozens of mules were snorting and stamping.

With no money left – they had agreed not to use any more of the gold coins unless matters were truly desperate – Felix and Livia couldn't afford one of the tiny rooms on the upper level of the main building where the more well-off traders and merchants slept, so they had opted instead to sleep outside.

'Be careful out here tonight,' said Merybad, who had taken a room for the night. 'And be sure to keep your valuables close.' He nodded towards a man with a big bald head, an enormous moustache and a large curved blade in his belt. Lowering his voice, he added, 'There are some unsavoury types around here.'

As the shadows lengthened across the courtyard, Felix and Livia unrolled a couple of rugs, wrapped themselves in their cloaks and prepared to sleep.

As usual, Big Nose (Felix was trying to remember to think of him by this name) was kneeling slightly apart from the other camels, who seemed to shun him.

Eventually, darkness fell and the activity in the courtyard ceased. But Felix found he couldn't sleep for the snoring people and farting camels, and the farting people and snoring camels. Finally, he sat up.

'What are you doing?' Livia murmured.

'I need to get some fresh air,' Felix told her.

Livia waved a hand in front of her face. 'I know what you mean.'

They picked their way between the groups of slumbering animals and people until they reached a dark, deserted corner of the caravanserai. There they perched on the edge of a disused water trough, now empty.

'Have you ever seen so many stars?' Felix marvelled, gazing up at the sky speckled with pinpricks of light.

Livia tugged at his sleeve. 'Someone's coming,' she whispered.

Felix lowered his eyes to watch the flicker of a lantern approach from the far side of the courtyard. When the light caught a gleam of bald head and curved blade, he drew in his breath sharply. 'Merybad warned me about him,' he said.

'Let's go back to the camels,' Livia suggested.

'Too late,' said Felix. 'He's coming this way. Quick – we can hide in the trough.'

They scrambled into the dry trough just as the pool of light cast by the man's lantern reached their corner.

Huddled against the cold stone, Felix listened to the scuff of footsteps as the man paced around. What was he doing out here?

Long minutes passed and Felix felt his muscles starting to cramp. Would the man never leave? Felix only realised the man must have been waiting for someone when he heard a gruff voice say: 'You're late.'

'I'm sorry, Narseh – I had to wait until I could be sure I wasn't seen,' said a second man.

That voice … Felix felt Livia shift next to him.

'Merybad,' she breathed in his ear.

'So what did you want to show me?' the gruff man asked.

'This.'

There was a pause, then the gruff man let out a low whistle.

Unable to suppress his curiosity, Felix peered over the lip of the trough.

Merybad was holding out a coin.

The man with the sword was peering at it. 'That looks like gold,' he said.

'It *is* gold, but that's not the point.' Merybad tapped the coin with his finger. 'Look at the symbols on the front and back.'

Narseh took the coin and held it close to the lamp. 'That's Cleopatra, isn't it?' He flipped the coin over. 'And on the other side is Caesar.' He raised his eyes to Merybad. 'What does that mean?'

'I'll tell you what I think, as incredible as it sounds. Have you heard the rumours about Caesar's treasure?'

The bald man brought his enormous eyebrows together in a frown. 'You mean the special treasure he plans to display during his triumph? I heard that it was stolen from a prefect in Belgica and then lost in a shipwreck.' His face creased in mirth. 'I bet Caesar will be feeding that prefect to the ostriches!'

'Yes, yes, I'm sure the ostriches will find him very tasty,' Merybad said impatiently. 'I heard that too. But what if that story was a mere decoy, designed to throw thieves off the scent of the real whereabouts of the treasure?'

Narseh's frown deepened. 'I don't follow you,' he said.

'Listen,' Merybad said. 'As I was leaving Alexandria, I was approached by two young Romans who were in a great hurry to leave the city, just ahead of a patrol searching for a pair of thieves. Now it so happens that while in Alexandria I heard talk of a special coin commissioned by Cleopatra as a gift for Caesar. And—' the trader took the gold coin from the swarthy man's outstretched palm '—the young Romans paid me with this.' He turned the coin between his fingers, a calculating look on his face. 'Have you ever seen such a coin before? I haven't – I think it's a *very special* coin.' His eyes shifted from the coin to the bald man. 'I think they are carrying *Cleopatra's gift to Caesar.*'

Narseh rocked back on his heels. 'You think your two young nobodies stole Caesar's gift?'

'How else do you explain this?' Merybad argued, holding the coin so that it caught the light from the lantern.

Narseh reached for the coin again, but Merybad closed his fingers around it. 'Wouldn't it be a pity if more experienced thieves should steal those coins from the original thieves?' he murmured.

The two men snickered.

'What are you thinking?' asked Narseh. His free hand went to the sword at his belt. 'Should I slit their throats as they sleep?'

Instinctively, Felix put a hand to his throat. Beside him, Livia smothered a gasp.

'No,' said Merybad thoughtfully. 'We need to be more subtle than that. No suspicion can fall on me. Other travellers on the road will have seen me with the young Romans. But if our caravan was to be attacked, and the poor young travellers were to be …' The trader ran a finger across his throat.

The bald man grinned. 'We can share the treasure.'

'Exactly. So, let us agree to meet again two days from now, on the plains outside Tadmor.'

'You're very bad, Merybad,' said the bald man in an appreciative tone.

The trader smirked. 'And you're very nasty, Narseh.'

Felix watched over the lip of the trough as the two men made their ways separately across the courtyard, then he stood up, wincing as he stretched his cramped limbs.

'Did you hear that, Livia? Those coins are meant for Caesar!' He shook his head in despair.

Livia stood up too. 'We have Cleopatra's gift for Julius Caesar!' she said with wonder in her voice.

Felix covered his face with his hands. 'Oh no,' he said. 'Oh no, no, no. This is terrible. I run away from the army, help one of the governor's slaves to escape from a prefect's household, and now I've stolen Caesar's gift. When we get back to Rome, Caesar will definitely feed me to the lions. Or the ostriches.'

But Livia's eyes were shining. 'This is *great*. Don't you see? We can return Caesar's coins in exchange for my brother's life.'

'That's if we make it to Rome alive,' Felix pointed out. 'Did you see the big sword that Nasty man was carrying?'

Livia looked grim. 'That *is* a problem,' she agreed. 'What are we going to do?'

Felix thought for a minute, absently rubbing the ring on his thumb. They had no weapons with which to confront the men, only the stick he had carried from the *Tarshish*, and that would be no match for

Nasty's sword. 'The only thing I can think of is that tomorrow night, while Merybad is asleep, we'll take Big Nose and escape.'

Livia looked even more grim. 'I don't know if I feel quite comfortable trusting our lives to Big Nose,' she said.

Felix shrugged. 'He's the only camel who'll help us.'

They returned to their beds in silence.

It was a long time before Felix fell into an uneasy sleep, and it seemed like only minutes later that he was woken at dawn by the jingling of harnesses and stamping of hooves on flagstones, the mingled noises of humans and animals as the caravanserai came to life.

As Felix stretched and yawned, Merybad arrived, beaming at them with more warmth than he had shown previously. 'I trust you slept well? Nothing disturbed your slumber? Your, er, belongings were not tampered with?' He gestured to the satchel sitting on the ground by their feet. Livia picked it up and slung it over one shoulder.

'We slept very well,' she said. 'But we're looking forward to resuming our journey. How far is it to Tadmor from here?'

Merybad stroked his beard. 'Perhaps three days. But we will need to take care; I have heard there are bandits in the area preying on unsuspecting travellers.'

Felix tried to appear suitably shocked. 'Oh no. Will we be okay?'

Merybad smiled and gave a little bow. 'Trust in Merybad,' he said, 'and everything will be fine.'

Felix forced himself to return the smile. 'I'm glad we're travelling with you,' he lied.

The day passed like so many others, trudging through the barren landscape, the only difference being that every stunted tree they saw on the horizon looked to Felix's anxious eyes like a bandit about to pounce, and his pulse raced every time they passed an outcrop of rocks, half expecting Nasty to leap out from behind with his sword raised.

It was an effort to converse normally with Merybad as they ate their simple evening meal, but finally it was time to arrange themselves for the night.

When at last they heard the faint snuffling that meant the trader was asleep, Felix touched Livia lightly on the arm and they rose silently. Felix picked up his stick and Livia lifted the satchel, and they crept between two camels.

'Shah!'

Felix froze. Merybad had spotted them!

But then the snuffling resumed, and he realised the trader was merely driving the camels in his dreams.

Hurrying to where Big Nose slept, Felix was glad of the camel's habit of sleeping apart from the others.

'Big Nose, wake up,' he whispered, placing a hand on the sleeping camel's neck.

'Okay!' said the camel, immediately alert.

'Shhh,' Felix hushed him.

'Okay!' said the camel at the same volume.

'Merybad has been plotting with a nasty man to kill us tomorrow and we need to escape,' Felix explained quickly in a low voice. 'Will you help us?'

'Okay!'

Felix and Livia climbed aboard, Felix in front, then the camel clambered to its feet.

It stood without moving.

'Tell the camel where to go,' Livia suggested.

Felix bent to speak into the camel's ear. 'Um, could you take us to Tadmor, please?' he asked.

'Okay!' the camel replied. But he still didn't move.

'Do you know where Tadmor is?' Felix asked, with a rising sense of panic.

'No,' the camel admitted regretfully.

Felix dropped his head onto the camel's furry neck. Now what? They couldn't just wander randomly through the desert – they'd die of starvation or dehydration within days.

Felix let out a low moan, which was interrupted by Livia.

'That star there – that's the North Star. I was trying to work out which direction we were travelling in today, and from the movement of the sun I'm pretty sure we've been heading north, so all we need to do is follow the star.'

Felix quickly relayed the instructions to the camel, which obediently began to plod towards the beacon in the sky.

'You're brilliant, Livia!' Felix said.

Eventually the stars faded from the sky and the sun began its ascent. As the pale sand turned a deeper gold with the changing light, Felix grew increasingly uneasy. The desert was now an endless flat expanse; there were no crags behind which they could hide, no dunes in which they could conceal themselves. If Merybad was in pursuit, he would have no trouble finding them.

It was mid-afternoon when Felix thought he heard a faint sound from behind. Turning, he scanned the horizon in the direction they had come. He thought he spied something moving, just a speck in the distance, but it was hard to tell with the sun beaming down, making the sand shimmer.

'Livia,' he said, 'take a look behind us. I think there's—'

'What's that?' Livia broke in. She was pointing ahead.

'What?' said Felix, blinking. His eyes were still dazzled from the sun on the sand behind them.

'I saw a glint. Or maybe it was a gleam.'

'Well, which was it?' Felix asked a little impatiently, casting another glance over his shoulder. Was the speck behind them getting nearer?

'Maybe it was both,' said Livia uncertainly. 'The glint of a sword *and* the gleam of a bald head.'

That made Felix swing his gaze forwards. 'Where?'

Livia pointed again.

At first Felix couldn't see anything, then – yes, he had it. A flash, as if the sun had just struck the blade of a sword … or a bald head.

'We should have thought of that,' Livia said grimly. 'Nasty would have had to go on ahead if the plan was for him to confront us as we approached Tadmor. We'll have to take a different direction.

Maybe if we head west to the coast we could then continue north to Tripoli and avoid Tadmor altogether?'

She turned to check the desert behind them. 'Oh!'

Felix, who was still watching the spot where he'd seen the glint (or gleam), spun around.

The speck was larger now, and growing more distinct by the minute.

Livia stifled a cry of alarm.

'Merybad!'

Despite the warmth of the day, a cold feeling invaded Felix as he realised the hopelessness of their situation: Merybad gaining on them quickly from behind, Nasty coming towards them ...

Felix faced forwards again to see if Nasty had moved closer, but instead of a gleam (or glint) he noticed something peculiar happening up ahead: a huge cloud hung over the horizon.

'Livia, look,' he said urgently, pointing.

Biting her lip, she turned away from Merybad. When she saw the cloud, she frowned. 'That's weird. It doesn't rain in the desert, does it? So why would there be a cloud?'

'What's weirder,' Felix observed, as he felt the first stirrings of a breeze brush his skin, 'is that it's the exact same colour as the sand.'

As the stirrings grew stronger, he realised with horror that the cloud was approaching quickly, barrelling along the sand like the waves that had engulfed the *Tarshish* all those weeks ago.

'What's happening?' Livia asked anxiously as Big Nose seemed to sway beneath them.

Without a word, the camel dropped to its knees and rested its head on the desert floor as if to sleep.

'I think it must be a sandstorm,' Felix replied, clambering off the camel's back. 'Should we turn around?'

'There's no point,' Livia said, as she too dismounted. 'It's coming so fast, we'll never outrun it. And we'll be heading straight for Merybad. Is there somewhere we can hide?'

Felix gestured to the vast empty space about them. 'There isn't anywhere.'

He had to shout now to be heard over the shrieking wind. The sand was whipping at his face.

'Let's try to head west,' Livia called.

'Okay,' he replied. 'Which way is that?'

The sun had disappeared completely. He couldn't see the sky, couldn't see ahead of him, couldn't see behind. Sand was whirling everywhere, finding its way into his eyes, nose, his mouth, his ears.

'Livia!' he shouted. 'Which way is – Livia? Where are you?'

He heard a whimper and looked around desperately, but he couldn't catch so much as a glimpse of his friend. She had disappeared into the swirling sands.

'Here!' he heard. 'This way!' But the voice wasn't hers, he realised, with a rising sense of panic.

He stumbled backwards into the camel and fell onto the sand.

'Livia, run!' he yelled, not caring who heard him. 'Don't worry about me!'

He might be trapped, but all he wanted was for her to get away.

'Run!' he screamed again as he felt someone seize him by the arms and drag him to his feet.

'Let go,' he said, struggling with all his might and trying to lash out with his stick.

'Stop!' said his captor firmly, holding Felix tightly so his arms were pinned to his sides. 'I'm trying to help you.'

'What?!'

Felix felt his feet leave the ground. He was being carried. By whom?

'Where are you taking me?' He tried to wriggle free from his captor's grasp.

Abruptly he was released. He was standing on solid ground once more, and the awful swirl of sand, the roar of the wind, had ceased. Everything was calm.

'Welcome to our tent.' It was his captor's voice –
but it didn't belong to Merybad or Nasty.

Blinking sand from his eyelashes, Felix could just
make out the entrance to a tent and a tall, slender
man with a scarf covering his face, leaving a narrow
slit for the eyes.

'Be calm,' the man said. 'You are safe now.'

'My friend,' Felix croaked, his throat dry from the
dust. He stumbled towards the entrance. 'I have to
find her.'

'Here.' He felt a tug on his cloak and turned with
a rush of relief to see Livia. 'Felix, it's okay, I'm here.'

As the adrenalin drained from his body, Felix sank
to the ground, spent of energy.

Looking up, he saw he was surrounded by a dozen
or so curious faces: young, old, boys, girls, men and
women, sitting and kneeling on the carpets that
covered the sand.

'I am Hatem,' the man who had brought Felix
into the tent told him. 'And this is my family.' He
went around the circle, introducing his guests to sons
and aunts, grandfathers and daughters and cousins.
'Rest with us a while. The storm will soon blow
over.'

'Our camel,' Livia said anxiously. 'Will he be all
right out there?'

'He'll be fine,' the man assured her. 'Our own camels are there, and our goats. Like us, they are accustomed to the weather. But you, perhaps, are not?'

'No,' Felix admitted. 'It's our first time crossing the desert.'

'Where are you headed?' Hatem asked.

'We're on our way to Tadmor. Do you know if we're close?'

'You're very close. We will be passing near there ourselves.'

'Where have you come from?' Livia asked.

A woman – Uzza, Felix recalled – laughed and gestured around her. 'This is our home.'

'You live in this tent permanently?' Felix asked, puzzled. He had to admit, though, it was a large and comfortable-looking tent, the woven fabric draped over wooden poles protecting them from the swirling sands outside, a small fire in the centre of the space adding to the cosy feel.

'We're nomads, goat herders. We move through the desert, occasionally visiting towns to sell our milk and cheese.' Something in Felix's expression must have betrayed his hunger, because she smiled and said, 'When the storm blows over, we will prepare you a feast.'

'That would be wonderful,' Felix said, 'but, um, we're in a bit of a hurry ...' He glanced around as if he might see Merybad, or perhaps Nasty, through the skin of the tent.

Hatem, who was standing by the tent flap, turned and gave him a penetrating look. 'Do not worry, young friend. You are safe with us.'

Felix grimaced. 'You don't understand,' he began. 'There are two men out there who—'

He stopped as the nomad family rose as one. In the time it took Felix to blink, every member of the family had produced a weapon: a sword here, a knife there ... even a woman who appeared old enough to be Hatem's grandmother wielded a large wooden club. They seemed fierce, Felix noted, but not threatening.

'You are safe with us,' Hatem repeated. 'No one will harm you here.'

He sounded very sure, Felix thought. Before he could ask if Hatem knew Merybad and Nasty, the nomad opened the tent flap and peered out. 'See? The storm has passed, though night is falling.'

Felix and Livia stepped outside into a cool, clear evening.

Immediately, Livia said, 'Our camel has gone! He must have been frightened by the storm. Oh, the poor thing.'

At Felix's questioning look she said, 'I might find him frustrating at times – okay, always – but I *do* know he means well.'

'Don't fret,' Hatem soothed her. 'He has probably joined his fellows.'

Felix frowned. 'What fellows?' He felt a jolt of alarm. 'You mean Merybad's other camels?'

'This way,' Hatem said calmly, leading Felix and Livia around the side of the tent. As they walked, the nomad said, 'Whispers carry on the desert breeze and travellers will tell tales. I think you have come from Alexandria, hmm?'

'Yes,' Felix said warily. He noticed Livia tighten her grip on the satchel she carried.

'And you stayed in a caravanserai the night before last?'

'Yes,' Felix admitted reluctantly.

'Perhaps I have heard talk of you. But that is of no importance. What matters to me is that when we offered you shelter you both thought first of each other's safety and were concerned for your camel.'

'Well, our camel is quite sensitive,' Felix explained. 'And I'm not sure how smart camels usually are, but he seems particularly – oh, there he is, standing with the others.'

A small herd of camels was grouped in the lee of a large rock, and in their midst was Big Nose.

Felix watched as the other camels nuzzled Big Nose affectionately. He had never seen the camel look so happy.

'As I was saying,' Hatem resumed, 'your concern for each other and your camel tells me everything I need to know about you. My family and I would be pleased to take you to the outskirts of Tadmor.'

'Thank you,' Felix said. It was like a weight had been removed from his shoulders. For once, it seemed, things were going their way.

That night they ate goat roasted on the fire, accompanied by side dishes of vegetables, many of which were strange to Felix. They slept on the carpet-strewn floor of the tent, and the next day they walked with the nomads to the oasis city of Tadmor.

Chapter 16

'**D**o you think Big Nose will be happy with the nomads?' Felix knew that leaving the camel with the herd that had made him feel so welcome was the right thing to do, yet he couldn't help but feel that they'd abandoned him – just like they'd abandoned the sacred chicken in Lutetia. He still suspected that if they hadn't left the chicken behind things might have turned out very differently. He twisted the ring on his thumb. They'd probably be in Rome by now, for one thing.

'You're thinking of that silly chicken again, aren't you?' Livia demanded.

'Maybe,' Felix said defensively.

'The chicken left us, we didn't leave him,' Livia pointed out. 'And the camel will be much happier with the nomads than he was with Merybad.' She wrinkled her nose as she spoke the name of their would-be murderer. 'Besides, it's not like we could take a camel to Rome with us.'

They were in Tadmor, walking through a marketplace unlike any Felix had seen before. There were fortune tellers and scribes, spices whose scents made his nostrils widen and shrink – and was that a snake charmer? Perhaps Gisgo's tales hadn't been so fanciful after all ...

It was true they couldn't take the camel all the way to Rome, but perhaps they would have been wise to ride him to Tripoli. Hatem had estimated it would take them ten days to reach the port on foot. Their chances of reaching Rome in time to see Livia's brother were growing fainter and fainter, though Felix couldn't bring himself to point that out to Livia, who was as determined to get there as ever.

Livia clutched his arm so tightly Felix let out a chicken-like squawk. 'Hey!' he said.

'It's him,' she hissed. 'Nasty.'

Looking around, Felix spied their pursuer moving through the crowd just as the big bald man spotted him.

With a roar, Nasty charged towards them.

'Quick, Livia – this way!' Felix yelled.

They took off at a sprint down a street lined with textile merchants. As they ran, Livia pulled over some bolts of cloth. Nasty was forced to slow down to navigate them as they rolled into his path.

The street opened out into a square filled with market stalls piled high with fruit and vegetables, cheeses and baked goods. They ducked and weaved down the aisles, apologising to startled shoppers as they went.

At the far side of the square, Felix stopped short. 'Livia, look – this shop is called Sami's Sacred Carpets and the sign has a golden chicken painted on it.'

Livia, who had continued running, raced back to grab Felix by the arm. 'Come on,' she urged. 'We don't have time to shop.'

'But it might be a good omen,' Felix argued.

Livia tugged on Felix's arm. 'Not now,' she said impatiently. 'We need to find somewhere to hide.'

Felix stepped forwards, dragging Livia with him, until they were both standing on a carpet draped over the dusty street. 'Cleopatra hid inside a rolled-up carpet,' he said excitedly. 'Wouldn't it be great if we could do the same?'

At once the carpet began to shake violently beneath them, and Felix and Livia were both flung to the ground.

'What is it?' Livia cried. 'An earthquake?'

Before Felix could respond he found himself being turned over and over. He felt an elbow in his nose and a knee in his stomach, as if all the sharpest parts of Livia were being jammed into the softest parts of Felix. It must be an earthquake, he decided, except … The turning ceased. He was wrapped in the coils of the carpet, unable to move, but by shifting his eyes back in their sockets he could just see a circle of light, and in that circle he had a glimpse of the square through which they had run. He heard a grunt, then Livia said, 'I think my chin is stuck under your armpit.'

'Ssshh,' Felix responded. 'Here comes Nasty.'

The bald man was lumbering through the market, elbowing people out of the way, swivelling his head from left to right as he searched for Felix and Livia.

'What's he doing?' Livia whispered.

'Pushing over an old woman's cart full of grapes and yelling at her.'

A crowd was gathering now. Nasty tried to fight his way through but he was surrounded. Felix could hear him bellowing like an outraged bull as the crowd slowly pushed him back, back, out of the square.

'He's gone,' Felix said at last.

'Good,' said Livia. 'Your plan worked. I wish you'd given me some warning, though – I didn't know what was going on.'

'It wasn't *my* plan,' Felix said.

'And did you have to roll the carpet so tight? I feel like I'm being strangled. If Nasty really has gone, you can loosen it.'

Abruptly the carpet unfurled.

'That's better,' said Livia as they lay somewhat dazed on the carpet, which was flat once more. 'Now, what were you saying?'

'I said it wasn't *my* plan. Livia, I think ...' Felix hesitated. What he was about to say sounded ridiculous. 'I think the carpet did it. I think the carpet can understand us.'

'That sandstorm yesterday was very disorientating,' Livia said with concern. 'Perhaps you're still a little dizzy.' She sat up and reached into the satchel for the waterskin. 'Here, drink some of this. Does your head hurt?'

Felix waved the flask away. 'I'm serious, Livia. I had nothing to do with what just happened. The carpet did it on its own.'

'What are you saying? That you think it's a—' she glanced up at the sign with the golden chicken '—a sacred carpet?'

Felix raised his palms. 'Maybe not sacred, but it could be a *magic* carpet. Remember what Gisgo said on the *Tarshish*? He'd seen carpets that could fly.'

'You didn't actually believe his stories, did you? He also told us he'd seen mermaids, remember? And snake charmers.' Her mouth dropped open, and Felix guessed that she was remembering the snake moving to the music of a flute in the bazaar they'd walked through.

'I think he was telling the truth,' Felix persisted. 'Who would make up such a thing as a flying carpet?'

As he spoke, he felt a slight rocking sensation. Once again, he feared an earthquake, but no – the movement wasn't that strong; it was barely a tremor. Then he realised what it was. Slowly, almost imperceptibly, the carpet was rising. Felix stared at the ground, incredulous.

'Livia,' he said, pointing.

She was still talking. 'Okay, so he might really have seen a snake charmer, though that stuff about mermaids and sea monsters was definitely made up. And I can tell you one thing for sure: there is no such thing as a magic carpet.'

Unexpectedly, they started falling. The carpet had tipped them off!

'Are you quite sure about that, Livia?' Felix asked, rubbing his knee where it had hit the ground.

Livia was silent, rubbing her hip. Finally, she said, 'Well, it's a cranky magic carpet.'

Their conversation was interrupted by a voice that matched the carpet for crankiness. 'What are you doing on my carpet? Go away!'

A short, wide man with dark, narrow eyes was glaring at them and making shooing motions with his hands.

'Fine,' said Felix, standing up. 'We won't buy your carpet. Come on, Livia.'

At once the crankiness was exchanged for a syrupy tone. 'Wait! You want to *buy* this carpet?'

'Felix ...' said Livia.

'Not anymore,' Felix told the carpet seller.

'I'll give you a good price,' the man said in a wheedling tone.

'How good?' Felix wanted to know.

'Well, not *that* good,' the seller hedged. 'After all, this is a very special carpet.'

Felix nodded knowingly. 'You mean it's magic.'

The man stared at him. 'Magic? What nonsense. There's no such thing as a magic carpet.'

'Then what's so special about it?' Felix asked, looking down. The carpet appeared quite ordinary to him, slightly worn, with geometric patterns in shades of red, blue and white.

'It comes from far, far away in Anatolia,' the seller replied. 'It was brought to me by a traveller who said it belonged to King Pharnaces II.'

'A likely story,' Felix said. If King Pharnaces II had a magic carpet, why had he been defeated by Caesar? 'It doesn't look like the carpet of a king. It's kind of shabby.'

The carpet rippled slightly, as if to disagree, and that decided him.

'Give me a gold coin, Livia.'

'What? No!' She hugged the satchel to her chest.

'Please.' Lowering his voice, he added, 'Before Nasty returns.'

Her eyes darted towards the market square and then, clearly reluctant to waste any more time, she reached into the satchel for the box of coins and extracted one. Reluctantly, she held it out for the seller to examine.

He raised his eyebrows appreciatively. 'Sold!' he declared. 'Young sir, young miss, you are now the proud owners of the carpet of King Pharnaces II.' As if fearing they might change their minds and demand the coin back, he hastily rolled up the carpet, thrust it at Felix and said quickly, 'Thank-you-for-shopping-at-Sami's-Sacred-Carpets-have-a-nice-day.'

They strode off down the street, Felix with the carpet under his left arm and clutching the stick with his right hand.

'What did you buy a carpet for?' Livia exploded. 'Are you seriously intending to walk all the way to Tripoli carrying a carpet? Well, don't expect me to help.' And she stalked off down the street, fuming.

Felix unrolled the carpet and stepped onto it.

'Okay,' he said. 'Let's go.'

Nothing happened.

'Fly!'

Still nothing. He was starting to feel a little foolish, standing on a carpet in the middle of the street.

'Please,' he begged. '*Please* fly.'

And then, just as he was beginning to doubt the carpet's powers, it slowly began to rise.

'Yes!' said Felix, jubilant. 'Can you catch up to Livia?' Then he added hastily, 'Please.'

Felix planted his legs wide apart for balance, and the carpet cruised slowly along the street just above the ground. They were gaining on Livia, gaining on her ...

'Whoa!' he cried.

Livia jumped, startled, as the carpet bumped her.

Spinning around, she fixed Felix with an aggrieved look. 'What did you do that for?'

She drew in her breath as she realised he was hovering several inches above the ground. She glanced at his feet.

'It must be some kind of trick,' Livia said suspiciously.

The carpet rammed her and she yelped.

'Okay, it's not a trick.' She rubbed her shin. 'Why does it have to be such a grump?'

'Stop being so rude to it,' Felix chided.

'All right, I'm sorry,' she said to the carpet. Then to Felix: 'But I still don't understand why you wasted one of Cleopatra's coins on it.'

'Because flying to the coast will be much faster than walking,' Felix explained.

Livia regarded the shabby carpet doubtfully. 'Do you really think this thing can get us all the way to Tripoli?'

In reply, Felix pointed up the street and said: 'Please, carpet, fly to the temple and back as fast as you can.'

The carpet took off at such a speed Felix was flung backwards. He had to cling on to the side as it careened down the street, stopped abruptly mere metres from the temple, then performed a wide sweeping turn before speeding back to where Livia stood gaping at them, her eyes wide in amazement.

'Now do you see why I bought the carpet?' Felix asked, unable to keep the smugness from his voice.

'Yes!' said Livia. 'I love the carpet!'

The carpet rippled with pleasure.

'Then what are you waiting for?' said Felix. 'Let's get out of here!'

Chapter 17

They flew day and night. It wasn't always comfortable. Sometimes the carpet dozed off and fell from the sky. Felix and Livia – asleep themselves – would be woken as they hit the ground with an almighty thump. They both had some rather nasty bruises as a result. Then there were the whirlwinds that came upon them swiftly in the desert, spinning the carpet in circles until they were all so dizzy they didn't know which way was which.

But these discomforts were a small price to pay, they agreed. After their escape from the Roman patrol in Alexandria and then from Merybad and Nasty in the desert, it was a relief to stop looking over their shoulders constantly. Plus, flying over the endless sands on a carpet was much more comfortable than travelling by camel or walking. 'And the carpet doesn't talk,' Livia noted with some relief.

Felix and Livia, meanwhile, had nothing to do *but* talk.

'You've told me about your mother and your sisters,' Livia remarked on the third day, 'but you haven't mentioned your father.'

It had been a long time since Felix had thought of his father. 'Dad was in the army, but he was killed in Armorica,' he explained. 'He was in General Porcius's legion too – that's why General Porcius gave me the post as his servant.'

Felix could hardly remember his father; he had laughed a lot and had a red beard, and he had called Felix 'Little Red' and said that one day Felix would have a red beard just like his own. But because he was a soldier, he had been away more often than he was home. After he died, Felix was so used to his father being gone that he sometimes forgot to miss him. He thought of General Porcius more often than his father these days, probably because he had spent so much more time with him. And he had been a good master; though the general was unlucky, he had never been unkind. For a moment Felix felt bad for letting him down. Then he recalled the Nervians.

As they soared across the desert under cloudless skies, it occurred to Felix that their return to Rome might not be quite so cloudless. In fact, both he and Livia were returning under a cloud. Desertion from the Roman army was a serious crime – though since he wasn't actually a soldier, and his desertion hadn't helped the enemy in any way, he could hope for mercy. While he no doubt had consequences to face, it was Livia he feared for the most. She was thinking no further ahead than freeing her brother (something that Felix thought privately might well prove impossible even for her – and that was if they made it to Rome in time), but what would happen to her next?

He was trying to decide whether to raise the subject with her when Livia let out a whoop of delight. 'Felix, look! Is that the sea?'

'We can't be there already,' Felix said.

But they were. Thanks to the carpet, the journey to the busy port of Tripoli had taken three days rather than ten. And within an hour of arriving at the docks Felix and Livia had secured passage on a ship bound for Ostia with a cargo of cereals and oil. From being hopeless, there was now a possibility they would reach Rome in time, though it would be touch and go.

'Our luck is changing,' Felix insisted as he heaved the carpet up the gangway of the *Minerva*; it seemed to grow heavier when it was tired. 'And it's all thanks to the sacred chicken.'

'The chicken?' said Livia, puzzled. 'How do you figure that?'

'Remember the shop where we bought the carpet? There was a golden *chicken* on the sign and it sold *sacred* carpets. That made me think of the sacred chicken, which is why I stopped. And that led us to the magic carpet.' He patted the rug affectionately.

'But I thought the chicken had cursed us, and that's why we've ended up so far off course?'

'Hmm, that's true,' Felix conceded. 'Maybe it means that wherever the chicken is now, it's happy, and the curse has been lifted.'

'Cursing? Who's cursing?' asked a small, round, weather-beaten man standing at the top of the gangplank. 'Get the flipper-fisted flounder over here. I'm the captain, and the only one doing the cursing on this ship is *me*.' He turned a protuberant pair of eyes on Felix and Livia. 'Who are *you*?'

'I'm Livia and this is Felix,' Livia reminded the captain. 'You agreed to take us aboard in exchange for two gold coins.'

'Oh yes, that's right,' said Captain Hanno. 'Welcome aboard, you jibbering starfish spleens!'

The funny thing about the cursing captain, Felix decided, was that he didn't seem like an angry or aggressive man. Rather, he seemed to take delight in the imaginative string of colourful curses he directed at random passers-by. And though Captain Hanno might be odd, his ship was a beauty. Instead of rowers, the *Minerva* relied on a single square sail and a complicated system of rigging to shear through the water at great speed – which was exactly what they were doing a week or so into their voyage, as Felix and Livia strolled the deck.

'So, if you're right, and the sacred chicken has blessed us,' said Livia, 'Caesar will be so glad to get these coins from Alexandria—'

'What's left of them,' Felix interjected.

'—that he'll release my brother and we'll live happily ever after.'

'Will you be freed from slavery?'

'Oh yes,' said Livia confidently.

Felix wasn't sure whether the coins were really so valuable, nor if the chicken's powers extended that far – though they might, he reasoned – but he was pleased to see Livia feeling so cheerful.

His pleasant musings were interrupted by an unwelcome cry from the crow's nest. 'Pirates on the starboard bow!'

Livia ran to the side of the deck with Felix close behind.

'No!' yelled Livia, pounding the rail. 'We don't have time for this! We need to get to Rome!'

One of the ship's mates came to lean on the rail beside them. He didn't seem in the least perturbed by the arrival of the pirates. 'Oh, don't worry,' he said. 'The captain will handle them.'

Sure enough, Captain Hanno was racing to the ship's side – and now he *did* look angry, Felix observed.

Roaring and red-faced, he waved his cutlass and let loose a string of curses.

'You flestering crab kidneys!

'Come on, you scrabulous anchovy lungs!'

The pirates on the advancing ship, who'd been roaring and red-faced themselves, grew silent as the captain's bluster increased in both volume and imagination.

'I'll have you, you bloopering octopus bladders!

'Attack me, will you, you snivelling scallop stomachs?!'

The cursing captain's crew watched on impassively.

'Pirates always seem to find the captain's tirades most unnerving,' the sailor near them said quietly out of the corner of his mouth.

The pirates seemed to shrink and shrivel under the captain's onslaught. Finally, a small, meek voice floated across the water from the pirate ship. 'Turn about.'

And the pirates turned their ship around and fled.

The rest of the voyage to Ostia passed without further incident, and they reached the port on a cloudy spring day. They were so close now, only fifteen miles from Rome.

Felix and Livia disembarked onto a quay lined with enormous two-storey warehouses, each painted with a sign advertising its business. Everywhere they looked, people were in motion. Amphorae of grain and olive oil were being ferried from ship to shore, while barrels of garum, the pungent fish oil, were transferred to barges that would transport them up the Tiber river directly to Rome. Outside a brick building painted with a lighthouse – the symbol of Ostia itself – they saw two men loading a cart with blocks of salt, probably cut from the salt flats just outside the town.

Livia approached them. 'Excuse me, when do Caesar's games start?' she asked.

'The games?' The nearest one waved a hand dismissively. 'Oh, that's all over.'

'It's over? You mean we missed it?' Livia threw Felix a panicked look. 'That means ...' Her face drained of colour.

The man on the far side of the cart pushed a block of salt into position then scratched his beard. 'Well, now,' he said slowly. 'That's not quite right. I don't think they've had the games yet. The third triumph finished three days ago, on the Ides of April, but there's still one more triumph to go.'

'Four triumphs in one month?' said his friend. 'That seems like a lot. I know Caesar routed the Gauls, and Ptolemy's forces in Egypt. What else is he celebrating?'

'Let's see. You're right, there was the Gallic triumph – he paraded Vercingetorix himself in chains. Then there was the Alexandrian triumph. Yesterday's was the Pontic; he sent Pharnaces II packing. So tomorrow he must be celebrating the triumph over Africa. And after that, of course—' the bearded man chuckled '—let the games begin!'

'The games ... they haven't held the games yet.' Livia clutched Felix's wrist as they walked on. 'We've made it. My brother is *alive*.' Her face was still pale, but her eyes were bright. 'Quick, we need to get to Rome as fast as we can. I'll find Caesar and give him the coins before the games start.'

'No problem,' Felix said. 'We can fly there on the carpet.' He patted the rolled-up carpet that sagged awkwardly over his shoulder.

'Great idea,' said Livia. She too patted the carpet.

'Let's wait till we're outside the gates of Ostia, though,' Felix suggested, 'so we don't draw too much attention to ourselves.'

They hurried down the Decumanus Maximus, the main street of the town, which was lined with apartment buildings and taverns and shops. A huge theatre stood alongside a square filled with the offices of merchants and shipowners, some decorated with mosaics of foreign harbours or faraway cities. Passing through the forum, Felix recognised a statue dedicated to Ceres, the goddess of grain, in the centre.

And then they were walking through the city gate and joining the road from Ostia to Rome. The Via Ostiensis was so thronged with travellers and traders it didn't seem possible to fly a magic carpet through their midst discreetly.

'But we don't need to stick to the road,' Felix pointed out. 'The carpet didn't need roads to find its way through the desert. We can fly over fields and forests.'

'It'll probably even be quicker that way,' Livia agreed.

Half a mile or so outside the town, they left the road and headed into a fallow field. There, they unrolled the carpet.

They both sat down, Livia with the satchel on her lap, and Felix tapped the carpet lightly with his stick. 'Take us to Rome, please, carpet.'

The carpet gave a reluctant heave, hovered for a few seconds barely an inch above the ground, then subsided.

'I think it's tired,' Felix said.

'Or lazy,' said Livia crossly.

The carpet gave a shudder that tipped her sideways.

'Hey!' she said.

'The carpet doesn't like to be insulted,' Felix reminded her.

'Hmph,' said Livia, folding her arms across her chest. Then she said contritely, 'I'm sorry, carpet. I'm just anxious to get to Rome to see my brother. But I shouldn't be taking my anxiety out on you.'

The carpet, as if in recognition of the apology, rippled gently and then gave another heave before sinking to the ground once more.

'That trip across the desert must have been too much for it,' Felix said. 'It's not a young carpet, after all.'

Livia turned a worried face to him. 'How will we get to Rome?' she asked.

'It's okay,' said Felix. 'We can go back to Ostia and use another of Caesar's coins to buy seats in a carriage.'

'I don't know,' said Livia. She had pulled the box of coins from the satchel and was counting them, looking troubled. 'We really should save the rest of the coins for Caesar. If there are too many missing he might refuse to free my brother.'

Felix looked at the sky, considering. The sun was still high; it wouldn't be dark for hours. 'It's only fifteen miles to Rome. We've walked that before easily. If we move quickly, we'll get there before dark. We could stay the night with Mum and then find Caesar during the triumphal procession tomorrow.'

Livia approved of this plan, and they set off at a good pace, but while the distance hadn't seemed far when they set out, as the miles passed slowly, and then more slowly, Felix realised he had been too optimistic. They took it in turns to carry the heavy carpet – though Livia suggested more than once that they should simply abandon it by the side of the road if it couldn't fly anymore. The carpet stuttered on her shoulder in what seemed like hiccupping sobs and she quickly apologised.

They trudged along, their flagging pace a contrast to the activity in the fields on either side of the road. Now that winter was well and truly over, farm workers were busy repairing fences and weeding crops, planting and pruning.

Just a little further, Felix told himself as they followed the march of aqueducts along the plain, carrying water to the great city founded by Romulus and Remus.

At last, as the first stars became visible in the dusky sky, they saw ahead of them the mighty square towers of the Roman gate known as Porta Ostiensis.

Felix let out a cheer. 'We made it!'

They hastened forwards, only to see two guards dragging a huge wooden gate across the opening.

'Wait!' shouted Felix, waving his stick. He began to run awkwardly, the carpet jostling on his shoulder.

But it was too late. The gate clanged shut.

Chapter 18

They made camp under the boughs of an oak tree in the middle of a field of cabbages, within sight of the walls.

'I can't believe we're eating cabbage leaves for dinner, when we could've been enjoying my mother's cooking,' said Felix in disgust.

'What would she have made for us?' Livia asked as she rolled up a leaf and bit into it.

Felix closed his eyes and imagined his mother standing over the charcoal brazier in the single room that served as the kitchen, dining room and living room in their cramped apartment. He pictured himself sitting at the table, the aroma from the cooking pot wafting over to him, the tantalising scent ... 'Cabbage soup,' he said.

When their meagre meal was complete, they unrolled the carpet and lay down to sleep.

'The carpet might not have been able to fly us recently, but it's been really comfortable to sleep on,' Felix observed as he stared up into the dark canopy of leaves.

The carpet, as if pleased by the compliment, vibrated gently beneath him.

'Maybe you could give it to your mother as a gift?' Livia suggested.

Felix laughed. 'I'll bet King Pharnaces II never thought his magic carpet would end up in an apartment in the Subura.'

Livia rolled over and propped herself up on her elbow. 'Is that where you live – the Subura?'

'That's right. Do you know it?'

Livia shook her head. 'I've heard of it, of course, but I've never seen it. The governor's mansion was on the Quirinal Hill.'

Rome's noble citizens tended to make their homes on various slopes of the city's seven hills, while the plebeians lived between the hills in quarters like the Subura, which was densely packed with apartment buildings.

'Where will you go ... after?' asked Felix, voicing the question that had been troubling him more and more as they grew closer to Rome. After *what*, he wasn't quite sure. Would Livia really be able to save her brother, and would Caesar really then liberate the pair of them, just for the sake of the handful of coins Livia had carried all the way from Alexandria?

'I don't know,' she replied softly. 'All I care about is seeing my brother. After that ...'

'Well, I'm sure my mother would let you stay with us,' Felix offered. It would be a tight squeeze, but he knew his mother would never turn down someone in need. Even his sisters had good hearts, really.

'I couldn't ask it of her,' said Livia. 'If Caesar doesn't free my brother, or he – he doesn't survive the arena ...' She paused then said, 'I'll have to go into hiding. Leave Rome. But whatever happens, I'm not going back to being a slave.'

'I'll help you,' Felix promised. 'In any way I can.'

She gave him a quick, grateful smile. 'I know.' She rolled onto her back again. 'If only I knew where I came from – where my parents were from, I mean – that's where I'd go,' she said. 'Maybe I even have a family out there in the world somewhere.' Her voice was dreamy now, close to sleep.

As Felix closed his own eyes and began to drift off he wished fervently that Livia and her brother would soon be free, and that they would find a home.

Woken by a startling noise, he opened his eyes to see that pale light was filtering through the fresh green leaves of the oak tree. Livia was standing by the carpet with her hands over her ears.

'What is that awful *sound?*' she shouted over the banging.

When the banging was overlaid with several loud blasts of a trumpet, Felix had his answer. 'It must be the musicians who are going to play in the triumphal procession,' he said. 'They'll be gathering in the Campus Martius waiting for the parade to begin.' The large field just outside the city walls was often used for public assemblies.

Felix stood up and brushed twigs and a stray cabbage leaf from his clothes then rolled up the carpet. He hoisted it over his shoulder – it was lighter now, he noticed, perhaps a result of all the rest it'd had – and picked up his stick, and they set off towards the gate that had been barred the evening before.

This time the gate was open, though there was a crush of people around it.

'Are all these people here to see the triumph?' Livia asked.

'Of course,' said an old woman next to her. Her hair was grey and she walked with a slight limp, leaning over a wooden walking stick. 'Everyone gets the day off work to come and watch. I'm too old to work now, but I've walked three hours each way from my village to come to all of them. I'm so old I can even remember the three triumphs of Pompey! His triumphs were ten years apart – not like Caesar, who has all his in the same month. Still, who can blame him, hey? It's a grand sight, a triumph.'

Livia put a hand under the old woman's elbow to support her as the throng carried them through the gate and along a street skirting the edge of the Aventine Hill.

'Look, it's the Temple of Diana,' said Felix, spying the familiar columns over the heads of the crowd. 'We're really here! In Rome!'

They passed between apartment buildings and shops, and were almost jostled into a stall selling fried fish on their left and then one offering snacks of salted peas on their right. Felix took it all in eagerly – the cries of peddlers, the excited chatter of the crowd anticipating the spectacle, the smell of meatballs and chickpea fritters.

'Will the procession come this way?' Livia asked the old woman.

'No, dear. They'll enter through the Porta Triumphalis then go through the Circus Maximus, around the Palatine Hill, along the Via Sacra to the Forum Romanum and finish by climbing the Capitoline Hill to the Temple of Jupiter.'

'So we just need to find a position with a good view of the procession and then wait for Caesar to come past,' Felix told Livia.

The old woman chuckled. 'If you wanted a good view you should've got here yesterday. The people at the front of the crowd will have put up tents along the route and slept there overnight.'

They were nearing the Forum Boarium now. With a thrill of recognition Felix spied the round edifice of the Temple of Hercules Victor. That meant they weren't far from the Circus Maximus.

'Maybe we could find our way up to a rooftop?' Felix suggested. But when he tilted his head back to look, he saw that the rooftops were as crammed with people as the streets.

'We need to be close to the procession,' Livia objected, 'if we're going to speak to Caesar.'

'Speak to Caesar?' The old woman hooted. 'You'll be lucky if you catch a glimpse of the wheel of his chariot through this mob.' Then, relenting at the sight of Livia's crestfallen expression, she said, 'You stick with old Balbina and I'll see you have a good spot. I've learned a trick or two in my time.'

Then, with a determination that belied her years and seeming frailty, she carved her way through the crowd with a mix of cajoling and curses and the deft application of her walking stick to bare toes. Livia and Felix, following in her wake, were subjected to a retaliatory onslaught of pointed elbows and bony knees.

The old woman stopped by a statue near the corner of the street that led from the forum to the Circus Maximus. It was Hercules, wearing the skin of the lion he'd slayed, a club resting over his shoulder rather like the carpet sagging over Felix's own shoulder.

'Here,' she said. 'Help me climb up onto the base of the statue and then you can join me. We'll see everything from up there.'

The base of the statue was a few feet off the ground. It would give them a good view, but Felix was hesitant. 'Stand on the pedestal of the divine Hercules?' he asked. 'Are you sure we're allowed?'

Balbina dismissed his concerns with a wave. 'No one's going to care today.'

So Felix scrambled onto the statue's base, then he pulled and Livia pushed the old woman into place before Livia clambered up to join them.

The noise of the assembled onlookers grew louder, but it was drowned out by drums as the procession neared. Looking over the top of the crowd, Felix saw a line of men in chains.

'They're the captives from Africa,' the woman said with satisfaction. 'King Juba himself isn't there. He died already, more's the pity. I would've enjoyed seeing him torn apart by lions in the arena.'

Felix shuddered. The old woman was surprisingly bloodthirsty.

He glanced at Livia. Her lips were pressed together in a tight line as she stared at the shackled captives. Some still bore the injuries of the battles they'd fought and lost. They all looked downcast and helpless. Felix himself could hardly bear to see. It so easily could have been him, paraded before a crowd of Nervians hurling rotten vegetables and insults. Even old Balbina was jeering in the face of the captives' misery.

It was a relief when the next part of the parade approached.

'Here comes the loot,' the old woman said eagerly, a greedy glint in her eye.

Sure enough, there came a line of wagons on which were chests filled with gold and silver coins. Dozens of them – no, *hundreds* of them. And not just coins:

golden crowns and jewels and precious gems glinted in the spring sunshine.

The old lady crowed her delight but Felix felt his spirits sink. There was no way the coins from Alexandria would impress Caesar in the face of all this wealth.

Next came wagons bearing weapons and armour belonging to the peoples Caesar had conquered, and then huge paintings showing scenes from the battles. The biggest of all showed a man with a crown and sceptre lying dead on a battlefield.

'Take that, King Juba,' Balbina cried merrily, brandishing her walking stick.

Felix clutched his own stick, trying to repress the impulse to stamp the point of it on the old woman's foot. The triumph was splendid, just as the woman had promised, yet Felix couldn't help but feel ill at what it all meant. Those captives – they were all going to be slaughtered in the arena or turned into slaves. And all those riches ... did that mean the conquered people had been left with nothing? On their journey from Belgica to Rome, Felix had met people from many different lands, including some that had been conquered by Rome, and their citizens had often been kind to him and Livia. How could he celebrate victory over them?

Troubled, he glanced in the direction the captives had gone, and saw a man walking along the edge of the procession, scanning the crowd as if searching for something. He was moving purposefully, but in the opposite direction to the way the parade was going. The man reminded Felix of someone. He couldn't think who. He stared at the tall figure, as slender as a ...

'Livia,' he said urgently. 'I think I just saw Reedy!'

'Who?' said Livia vaguely. 'Is he a friend of yours? That's nice.'

'He's not a friend – he's one of the governor's men who captured you in Belgica.'

That got her attention. She turned her head to face him. 'What? Are you sure? Where?'

Felix pointed to where he'd seen the slender figure. 'He's right over ...' But there was no sign of him. 'He *was* there.' Felix frowned.

'Maybe you were mistaken?' Livia said hopefully.

'Maybe.' Felix had a dreadful feeling that he hadn't been.

Two white oxen were led past, their horns gilded with gold and decked in garlands of flowers.

'They're going to be sacrificed,' the old lady explained, then cackled as one of the oxen turned its head to snatch a pastry from the hand of an onlooker.

The senators and magistrates were passing them now, all on foot, and then the crowd further down the street began to cheer wildly, the cheer surging towards them like a wave.

'What's happening?' Balbina wanted to know, craning her neck to see.

Felix squinted. 'I think I can see a horse,' he said. 'Maybe more than one.'

'I do hope the bandits were kind to that poor horse,' Livia whispered unexpectedly.

At this reminder of Belgica, Felix remembered that he was meant to be looking out for Reedy, but as he turned his eyes on the crush of people below he knew it would be hopeless trying to identify anyone.

Anyone, that is, except for the distinctive figure in the high-sided chariot pulled by four gleaming white horses, drawing ever nearer as the cheers rose to a crescendo.

Julius Caesar!

Felix heard Livia gasp.

Rome's greatest general was a majestic sight. Dressed in purple robes embroidered with gold thread, a laurel wreath perched on his close-cropped hair, he gazed imperiously over the crowd. From time to time he raised an ivory sceptre topped with a gold eagle in acknowledgement of the cheers that greeted him.

A slave stood slightly behind and to one side holding a golden crown above his head. He seemed to be whispering in the general's ear.

'The slave is reminding him that he's a mere mortal and not a god,' Balbina explained.

Caesar didn't appear to be listening to the slave. He stared resolutely ahead, though once or twice he cast irritated glances over his shoulder at the soldiers marching behind. For following the chariot were ranks of soldiers, singing loudly and boisterously. To Felix's astonishment, he thought he heard the words *smelly old Cheeser*.

'What are they singing?' he asked the old woman.

'They're singing rude songs about Caesar so that the gods won't grow jealous of him.' She clutched Felix's sleeve. 'Oh, this is a good one!'

Straining his ears, Felix heard the line ring out:
'Old Julie Caesar has a big nose!'

It was a promising beginning, but he couldn't hear what came next because right next to his ear Livia shouted: 'Caesar!'

Jumping from the statue's base, she started pushing her way forwards through the crowd.

Felix lost sight of her for a moment, as she was swallowed by the mass of people, then she resurfaced, still calling, 'Caesar!'

Felix was shifting the carpet on his shoulder and tightening his grip on his stick, readying himself to jump from the statue's base and follow her, when he spied a quicksilver figure slipping through the throng. Reedy!

'Livia!' Felix bellowed.

But his voice must have been drowned out by the rowdy singing of the soldiers.

A nose like a crocodile,

A nose as long as the Nile.'

'Livia!' he roared.

Felix jumped from the statue and flung himself into the crowd, shoving past the onlookers, stepping on toes, elbowing people, poking them with his stick, using the carpet as a battering ram. 'Livia! He's behind you!'

Reedy was closing in on her, reaching for her. If Felix could just—

'Gotcha!'

Chapter 19

Felix gasped as he felt a hand close vice-like around his arm, and he looked up into the red face of Beefy.

Ahead of him, Livia was struggling to free herself from the grasp of Reedy, her calls to Caesar growing fainter and more plaintive.

As the men dragged them away from the crowd and into the relative quiet of the forum, Livia asked in a subdued voice, 'How did you find us?'

Reedy laughed. 'You think the governor didn't guess why you ran away? He knew you'd be coming here to find your brother.'

'And you're about to see him again, just like you wished,' Beefy added. 'You too, chariot thief.'

He jerked Felix's arm roughly. 'But you won't need a carpet where you're going.'

Reedy laughed. 'The Underworld!'

'You mean my brother is …' Livia hesitated before choking out the word: 'Dead?'

'Nah,' said Beefy. 'At least not yet. He's in the dungeon.'

'He'll be dead tomorrow, though,' Reedy said. 'Once the wild beasts have torn him limb from limb.'

'And torn you apart too,' Beefy added. He shook Felix crossly. 'I thought I told you to dump the carpet.'

Felix had no intention of leaving the carpet behind. He was hoping to put it to good use.

'Seeing as it's going to be the last night of my life,' he said as he surreptitiously slipped his stick within the carpet's folds, 'you could at least allow me something comfortable to sleep on in the dungeon.'

Beefy chortled. 'Fair enough, lad. The games will be even more enjoyable if you're well rested!'

'Why's that?' asked Reedy.

'It'll take the giraffes longer to run him down,' said Beefy ominously.

The dungeons beneath the amphitheatre at the edge of town were cold and dank and dark, with just a little light filtering through a grate high in the wall.

After the gate clanged shut behind them, Felix and Livia stood for a moment, blinking, as they took in their new surroundings.

There was no movement, no sound, but as Felix's eyes adjusted to the dim light he could make out shapes slumped on the narrow wooden benches that lined two sides of the cell.

Livia, who had been peering at the faces of the slumped figures, let out a cry. 'Marcus!'

A tall, thin figure leaped from his bench at the same moment, yelling, 'Livia!'

In two steps Livia closed the distance between them and flung her arms around a boy who was a little taller than her but had identical dark looks.

Although Marcus's face was grubby and his clothes were ragged, his face was aglow with pleasure. 'What are you doing here?'

'I came to rescue you,' Livia said excitedly. 'I ran away from the governor, and just wait till you hear how we got here! There was a shipwreck, and we went to Alexandria, and we crossed the desert on a camel, and—'

'Oh, Livia,' said her brother sorrowfully. 'I'm glad to see you – really, I am – but what were you thinking? You shouldn't have come. Now you're going to be eaten by crocodiles too.'

Crocodiles? Felix gulped, recalling the serpent-like creature with giant teeth he'd seen on the dock at Alexandria. He'd thought the ostriches were going to be bad enough.

'I know,' said Livia in a small voice. 'I didn't mean to get caught. But I had to see you, Marcus. And now Felix is going to die too, and it's all my fault.'

At the mention of his name, Livia's brother turned an inquisitive gaze on Felix. 'Who are you?' he asked bluntly.

'I'm a friend of Livia's,' said Felix. 'We met in Belgica.'

'Don't talk to me about Belgica,' a mournful voice said from the corner.

'Flavius here has come from Belgica,' Marcus explained.

A small, bald man in a shabby toga raised a weary hand. 'Flavius Dellius,' he introduced himself. 'I was given a cushy post in Belgica in reward for my brave actions at the Battle of Alesia.'

'It's a shame about the weather,' Felix commiserated. 'Other than that, though, it seemed like a nice place.'

'I was quite looking forward to coming to Rome,' Flavius said wistfully. 'I was going to present Caesar with a gift symbolising his conquest over the Gauls and help to celebrate his triumph.'

'How did you end up in here?' Livia asked.

'I lost the gift.'

'Gosh, that's a shame,' said Felix.

Flavius nodded. 'Caesar wasn't happy.'

'You think that's bad? I lost the sceptre of King Juba,' a second man added gloomily.

Felix peered at him through the near darkness. The voice was vaguely familiar. 'Who are you?'

The man leaned forwards. 'General Cassius Cluvius. I'd just arrived in Lutetia to take up a consulship in recognition of the part I played in the conquest of Africa. Then I received a message summoning me to Rome to deliver the sceptre of Juba to Caesar. I had passage on a ship, but at the last moment I decided not to take it. The ship went down in a storm and the sceptre with it. So instead of sitting by Caesar's side watching the games, I'm going to be *in* them.'

'Keep it down in there, you lot,' an angry voice interrupted. 'The ostriches are trying to sleep. And you should, too – you'll have a lot of running to do in the morning. You'd be amazed how fast leopards are.'

Leopards? Were they those creatures with stripes and big teeth, or did they have a pointed horn? Felix couldn't recall. It didn't really matter, he supposed.

He picked up the carpet and carried it to the side of the cell. It felt lighter than ever. He decided to take that as a sign that his plan would work. It *had* to work …

Thanks to the carpet they spread beneath them, Felix, Livia and Marcus were not as uncomfortable as they might have been when they settled themselves on the cold earthen floor to sleep. The other two prisoners stretched out on the hard benches. Still, no one passed a comfortable night. The roaring of the lions intruded into Felix's dreams, as did a strange clacking noise that he feared might be the crocodiles gnashing their teeth.

The early-morning hours were spent in pacing, and trying to guess what might be going on in the arena above judging by the faint cheers that reached their ears.

Felix had a sick feeling in his stomach that had nothing to do with anything he'd eaten – he'd had nothing since the cabbage leaves more than a day before – and everything to do with nerves. While Livia and her brother sat in a corner and murmured, and the two men recalled the highs and lows of their eventful lives in Caesar's service (this was the lowest point, they agreed), Felix was trying to plot their escape. It was difficult to plan, he was finding, when there were so many unknowns.

First, there were the animals themselves. What if they pounced as soon as Felix and his fellows entered the arena? That would give him no time to unroll the carpet.

Second, even if he did manage to unroll the carpet in time, would it be able to bear the weight of all five of them? He'd only known it to carry two people before, but he and Livia couldn't possibly fly off and leave the others to their fate. In any case, Livia wouldn't leave her brother, he was sure – and Felix couldn't leave Livia. No, the carpet would have to carry all of them or none.

His thoughts were interrupted by a rattling of the gate barring the cell.

'Not long now,' a guard called. 'The elephant battle is almost over, and you're on next.' He added gleefully, 'The lions will be good and hungry; we've been starving them for days.'

'What about the ostriches?' Felix asked in trepidation.

'Oh, the ostriches are especially ravenous.'

It wasn't long after that the gate creaked open.

'All right, you lot,' said the guard. 'It's time.'

Felix picked up the carpet and his stick, and Livia slung the satchel over her shoulder.

'Hey, you can't take a carpet into the arena,' a guard objected when Felix filed out of the cell behind the others.

'Leave him alone,' said a second guard. 'Can't you see he's just a kid? Let him have his special blankie.'

Felix's mind went numb as they entered the arena. His eyes were dazzled by the light after the hours in the dark cell, and his senses were overwhelmed by the sea of faces surrounding them on all sides and the deafening roar of the crowd.

From somewhere Felix thought he could hear the answering roar of lions, though he couldn't see any animals.

Now was the time, Felix thought, before the wild beasts were let loose. If his plan was going to work, he'd have to move quickly.

He took the rolled-up carpet from his shoulder, set it on the ground and grasped the stick.

'Livia,' he said. 'Let's—'

But before he could finish his sentence, a guard started barking orders. 'Line up, prisoners. Caesar wants a word with you.'

Two more guards approached and Felix barely had time to scoop up the carpet and carry it under his arm as he and the others were prodded into place before the box in which the dignitaries sat overlooking the stadium.

Then they were face to face with Julius Caesar, dressed in his ceremonial garb, a laurel wreath encircling his head. Felix could make out half-a-dozen senators in togas seated in the shadows behind him, and behind them some generals in uniform.

'You have been brought to this place because you have displeased me,' Caesar declared.

He glared at the five prisoners standing before him.

'You, Prefect Flavius Dellius, lost the ring of Vercingetorix.'

Flavius Dellius was a prefect? And he had lost a ring?

That was a coincidence. Felix glanced at the ring on his thumb.

The prefect raised his palms helplessly. 'I looked everywhere. Under the table, behind the couch ...'

Felix held up a hand. 'Excuse me,' he said.

Caesar had already moved on. 'You, Cassius Cluvius, were my right hand in Africa and I was prepared to make you my right hand in Gaul. But when I asked you to perform one simple task ...'

'Didn't you like the substitute gift?' the general asked in a wheedling tone.

'Your substitute gift is extremely irritating. And speaking of irritating ...' He turned to Livia's brother. 'You, son of an Iberian chieftain.'

Livia gasped. 'Did you hear that, Felix?'

Caesar continued, 'You have been sent to me by the governor of Nemetacum, and though you have done nothing personally to offend me, I found your father extremely annoying. I beat him in the end though ... didn't I?' He glanced at a man beside him for confirmation.

'Yes, Caesar,' the man agreed.

'And I conquered Iberia?'

'Yes, Caesar.'

'Well, why didn't I think to have a triumph for that too?'

'Maybe next month,' suggested his companion.

'Good idea.' Caesar addressed Marcus again: 'In the meantime, young man, you will be fed to the wild beasts to symbolise my conquest of Iberia.'

Finally, he turned a perplexed gaze on Felix and Livia. 'I have absolutely no idea who you two are.'

Livia declared: 'I am the daughter of an Iber—'

'Perhaps it's not a good idea to bring that up now,' Felix interrupted. 'Tell him about Cleopatra's coins.'

'Oh,' said Livia. 'The coins. Of course. Well, you see ...'

Felix quickly unrolled the carpet. Would it fly?

Squawk!

He looked up. Was there a chicken in the arena?!

Then he saw a flash of black feathers from the corner of his right eye. Spying a raven on the right was a good omen! With renewed confidence, he dropped to his knees on the carpet.

'I'm Livia,' Livia was saying. 'Though that's not my real name, of course. Not my *Iberian* name. And this is my friend—'

'FELIX!'

Huh? Felix, still on his knees smoothing out the carpet, paused and squinted up into the crowd. At first he saw nothing except an indistinct mass of faces, but then he noticed someone high up in the stands jumping up and down and waving their arms above their head. It was his mother!

Felix leaped to his feet. 'Hi, Mum!' He waved madly.

'Quiet!' Caesar snapped. He was leaning forwards. 'That carpet you're standing on, boy – where did it come from?'

'We bought it in Tadmor, sir.' Best not to mention that they'd used one of Caesar's own coins, Felix decided.

'But the carpet seller said it came from Anatolia originally,' Livia added.

'I knew it!' Caesar slapped the edge of the box in delight. 'That's Pharnaces's rug! I'd recognise it anywhere. After the Battle of Zela, when the Pontics were routed, I went to the camp of their king, who had fled. In the king's own tent, I stood upon this rug and composed a letter to a friend back in Rome. *Veni vidi vici*, I wrote. *I came, I saw, I conquered.*'

As Caesar was speaking, the ground beneath Felix's feet had begun to tremble. Had someone released the elephants? Were they stampeding?

No, Felix realised; it was the rug. It was vibrating, almost as if it were simmering with rage.

Caesar's delighted smile turned into a glare. 'And then the pesky rug threw me off and I fell and hurt my knee.' He smiled again. 'Now here it is, appearing as if by magic to celebrate my triumph over its master.'

The rug bucked and Felix fell over.

Caesar laughed. 'Ha! That's definitely the rug I remember. Bring it to me,' he ordered.

'This is perfect,' said Livia, stepping onto the carpet. 'We can fly up and present him with the coins of Cleopatra and ask him to free us all.'

Felix tapped the carpet with his stick. 'Take us to Caesar, please, carpet,' he said.

But the carpet wouldn't budge.

'I think it's sulking,' Livia said.

They stepped off the carpet again, and Felix quickly rolled it up and slung it over his shoulder.

Cassius Cluvius stepped forwards. 'May I see that stick you're carrying?' he said.

And all at once Felix realised where he'd heard that voice before. 'You're—'

'Don't keep Caesar waiting,' a guard snapped. He gave Felix a shove, and kept shoving, until Felix and Livia had reached the edge of the arena.

From there, another guard led them up the steps to the back of Caesar's box.

At the entrance, Caesar's companion beckoned to them. 'Bring that rug here, boy.'

Obediently, Felix started down a small aisle that ran alongside the rows of seats. He was almost to the front when he noticed movement from the corner of his eye. A chubby toddler sitting on the knee of a disgruntled-looking senator was wriggling and reaching for Felix's stick.

'What's that the young lad's after?' Caesar demanded.

'My stick,' said Felix.

The child was wailing now and waving its pudgy arms, hands grasping for the stick.

'Well, give it to him,' Caesar said impatiently.

Reluctantly, Felix handed it over. The minute the toddler had the stick in his hand his tears dried and he began to coo, waving the stick happily.

'Actually,' Felix said, 'I think that stick belongs to—'

At the same moment, the senator announced, 'This isn't a stick.' He dodged left then right as it narrowly missed striking his nose. 'It's a sceptre.'

'Really?' said Caesar, the carpet momentarily forgotten. 'Whose?'

'That's what I was trying to tell you,' Felix said, gesturing towards General Cassius Cluvius in the arena below.

'Why, I do believe it's Juba's!' Caesar said, peering at it. 'The boy must have recognised his father's sceptre.' He turned back to Felix and Livia. 'But I thought it was lost in a shipwreck. How did *you* come to have it?'

Felix and Livia exchanged glances. 'It's a long story,' Felix said.

'Of course it is,' cried a voice happily. 'And a thrilling one too, I'm sure. Caesar, I know these young people – and so do you!'

A slight man in a toga was pushing through the crowd of generals and senators.

Felix and Livia stared at him in amazement. 'It's Titus Magius!' Livia said.

There by Caesar's side stood the poet they had last seen exiled on an island. He was talking into Caesar's ear and Caesar was looking at Felix and Livia doubtfully. 'Are you sure it's them?' he asked.

The poet wore a broad smile. 'I'm positive,' he said. 'Caesar,' he announced, 'this is Felix and Livia.'

'What are you doing here?' Felix asked the poet, bewildered. Then, in a whispered aside, 'I thought Caesar had exiled you because of your poem.'

'Ah, yes, but then I had one of the fishermen from my island sail to the mainland carrying a new poem I had written. There, it was delivered to a friend who saw that it was brought to Caesar. It was a tribute to his many triumphs.' He put a hand to his heart, lifted his chin and proclaimed:

'There was a great general called Caesar
Who won the battle of Alesia.

He won Africa, Pontus—
Even Egypt did want us.
(Cleopatra said our manners did please her.)'

When he was done, Caesar applauded, and the senators and generals quickly joined in. 'A masterpiece!' Caesar declared.

'Bravo!' the others muttered dutifully.

Titus bowed graciously. 'Caesar sent a ship for me. And when I got back to Rome I started reading him the new epic I was working on – and he loves it!'

'You're writing again?' said Felix. 'That's great.'

Titus moved to stand between Felix and Livia, flung his arms across their shoulders and said: 'Here they are, sir – the boy and girl on whom my new epic is based.'

Caesar's eyes lit up. 'Excellent. It's one of your best ever, Titus, old fellow. It's a pity you weren't able to finish it.'

'Alas, I didn't know how their story ended,' the poet confessed.

Livia stepped forwards. 'I can tell you how the epic ends.'

But she was pushed aside as slaves marched down the aisle bearing platters of food.

A familiar voice said, 'Where's my cake? Caesar promised me cake.'

It couldn't be! Could it? Felix looked around. 'Did I hear a chicken?'

'Yes,' said Caesar sourly. 'That incompetent general down there was meant to bring me King Juba's sceptre and he gave me a sacred chicken instead.' He moved to the edge of the box and glared down at the general. 'I haven't had a moment's peace since.'

Felix froze. He recalled the conversation he'd overheard that night from the deck of the *Tarshish*: the general saying, *I don't have any cake – just this grain*, and the chicken replying, *But I don't want grain. I want cake.*

The general had refused to board the ship in Massilia because the sacred chicken wouldn't eat the grain – and then the *Tarshish* had sunk.

Livia tried again. 'The general may have failed, Caesar, but—'

She was interrupted by a loud squawk.

'Oh, for goodness sake,' said Livia, looking down. 'Not you again.'

She sounded disgruntled, but Felix was delighted. It was the sacred chicken – *their* sacred chicken – alive and well!

Chapter 20

'It's so good to see you!' Felix exclaimed, dropping to his knees in front of the chicken.

The sacred chicken looked him up and down. 'Do I know you?'

'It's me – Felix! We left the army camp in Belgica together. We stole a chariot. Were held up by bandits.'

The chicken shrugged. 'If you say so.' It peered over its shoulder. 'Where's my cake?' it demanded.

'When we last saw you, you were in Lutetia, with the sacred geese at the temple,' Felix continued.

'Oh, them,' said the chicken. 'I couldn't stay there. Do you know what they ate? *Mud* cakes. Looking for worms. Worms!' It twitched its beak in distaste.

'And grass – ugh! No, I decided to carry on to Rome after all.'

'How did you get here?' Livia asked.

'A general came to the temple to give thanks for Caesar's favour, and I told him I was a sacred chicken and I needed to get to Rome. I might have mentioned that if he didn't help me he'd be cursed. He wanted to go by sea, but I put a stop to that.'

So it really had been the chicken he'd heard refusing the grain in Massilia, Felix realised. And just as well it had, or General Cluvius may well have sunk with the *Tarshish*.

'I was worried about you!' he told the chicken. 'I'm sorry we left you behind.'

The chicken was done talking with Felix. It walked up to Caesar and pecked him on the leg.

'Ow!' said Caesar, attempting to swat it away.

'Where's my cake?' the chicken demanded.

'You can't just order me to give you cake.' Caesar drew himself up to his full height and glared down his long nose at the chicken. 'I am Julius Caesar.'

'And *I* am a sacred chicken,' the chicken reminded him in a lofty tone. 'So if you want your future battles to go well ...'

Caesar sagged. 'Somebody get the chicken a piece of cake,' he shouted crossly. Then, to himself,

'I don't know how much more of this I can take. General Cassius Cluvius deserves worse than being slaughtered by wild beasts for cursing me with this cursed chicken.'

'It can be demanding,' Felix sympathised. 'I should know: I travelled with the sacred chicken from Belgica to Lutetia.'

Caesar gaped at him. 'You mean this is *your* sacred chicken? The one from the epic?'

'It's not *mine*, exactly …' Felix said.

Caesar put a hand on Felix's shoulder. 'Your obstacles were even greater than I had imagined.'

'Well, I did kind of miss the chicken after we'd parted,' Felix admitted. Then, acting on the suspicion he'd had earlier, he showed Caesar the ring that was still jammed on his thumb. 'Luckily I had this to remember him by.'

Caesar grabbed his hand. 'This ring. Where did you get this ring?'

'In Belgica. It was burped up by the sacred chicken, who found it in the house of a prefect.' He turned and pointed into the arena. 'Prefect Flavius Dellius. This is *the* ring, isn't it? Vercingetorix's ring? With the chicken on it?'

Titus broke in to explain: 'It's not a chicken, Felix, it's a rooster. It's a pun, you see? The Latin *gallus* stands for Gaul, but it's also the word for rooster.'

'That's my ring!' said Caesar, sounding excited. He held out his hand. 'Give—'

His words were drowned out by a squawk.

'Would you stop interrupting me!' he thundered at the sacred chicken.

The chicken sniffed. 'Who's ruffled your feathers?'

'I've got a good mind to send you down to the arena. Speaking of which—' he gestured to Felix and Livia '—it's time you two were going. The crowd is getting restless. And the hippos must be hungry ...'

'Not to mention the ostriches,' a senator piped up.

'Go back?' Felix protested. 'To the arena?' He was struggling to prise the ring from his thumb.

The poet looked regretful. 'Really, Caesar, can't you cancel this part of the program?'

'Of course not. Rome's citizens are expecting a good show, and I am but their humble servant.' Caesar beckoned to the guards. 'Take these two back to the arena,' he ordered, pointing at Felix and Livia. 'And then – release the beasts!'

Felix and Livia looked at each other in horror. They had come so close to being saved ...

'I don't regret anything, Livia,' Felix said, clasping her hand.

'Me either,' said Livia defiantly. 'I found my brother and I made a friend. The last three months have been scary and sad and stressful – and the best time of my life.'

'I would have liked to hear the ending, though,' Titus piped up.

'What ending?' said Caesar, as the guards closed in.

'The ending of the epic,' said Titus. 'Really, it would be best if it were a happy one.'

'Oh yes,' Caesar agreed. 'I like happy endings. Especially when I save the day. Or conquer something.'

'I can tell you the ending,' Livia declared. She stepped to the edge of the box and spoke in a voice loud enough to carry to the audience in the stadium. 'Livia, daughter of an Iberian chieftain, and Felix, son of a brave Roman soldier, have undertaken a perilous journey to bring Caesar treasures that symbolise the great victories we are celebrating here today.'

The hubbub of the restless crowd faded as all eyes turned towards her.

'When at last they arrived in Rome, the two young heroes presented to Caesar …' She paused.

Everyone leaned forwards, even Caesar.

'The ring of Vercingetorix! Caesar, this ring represents your conquest of Gaul.'

She pointed to Felix who, with a mighty wrench, pulled the ring from his thumb and handed it to the great general.

Livia raised her voice again: 'And the two young heroes presented to Caesar ... the sceptre of King Juba!'

She looked meaningfully from Felix to the baby. Felix reached for the sceptre, but the baby began to whimper. Rather than risk annoying Caesar with the baby's cries, Felix held up the baby clutching the sceptre.

'This sceptre represents your conquest of Africa,' Livia intoned.

Felix hurriedly returned the baby to the lap of the senator, who accepted him with some reluctance.

Livia's voice rang out a third time: 'And the two young heroes presented to Caesar ... the carpet of King Pharnaces II!'

It took all Felix's strength to pick up the carpet, which was as heavy as if it were completely sodden. 'I'm sorry,' he whispered to it.

Staggering under the weight, he offered the carpet to Caesar, who gestured for him to drop it at his feet.

'This carpet represents your conquest of Pontus,' Livia told him loudly.

Then she reached into her satchel.

'And finally, the two young heroes presented to Caesar ... the coins of Cleopatra!'

Bowing her head, she offered Rome's greatest general the wooden box containing the remaining coins from Alexandria. 'Um, they're almost all there,' she murmured. Then, in her ringing voice: 'Caesar, these coins represent your conquest of Egypt.'

Caesar opened the box and peered at the coins. 'These are from Cleopatra? Really? Oh look, I'm on one side and she's on the other. Isn't she pretty?' The great general sounded like a love-struck boy.

The arena was filled with cheers.

'Great is Caesar!

'Caesar victorious!

'Hurrah for Rome!'

Livia held up her hand for silence. 'In return, Caesar freed Felix and Livia. And he freed the son of the Iberian chieftain, Prefect Flavius Dellius and General Cassius Cluvius.' She gestured to the prisoners in the arena. 'That, Caesar, is how the epic ends.'

The cheering in the stadium continued, but those in the box had fallen quiet, all eyes on the great general.

Felix realised he was holding his breath.

Livia appeared calm, but behind her back her fists were clenching and unclenching.

Titus Magius cleared his throat. 'That would be a wonderful ending indeed. I'd love to write it. And people through the ages will know of Caesar the magnanimous, Caesar the merciful.'

The silence stretched until Felix thought he might faint from the strain.

At last, Caesar nodded.

'You speak very well for a slave girl,' he remarked to Livia.

'Rome may have made me a slave,' she said with a proud tilt to her chin, 'but I was born the daughter of an Iberian chieftain.'

Caesar stepped to the edge of the box and faced the crowd.

'I, Caesar the magnanimous—'

Squawk!

'Not now,' Caesar snapped at the sacred chicken. 'Can't you see I'm addressing the people of Rome?'

The chicken sniffed. 'So am I.'

Turning back to the crowd, Caesar tried again: 'I, Caesar the merciful—'

Squawk!

Without looking down, Caesar aimed a kick at the chicken.

He pointed to the three prisoners in the arena. 'Release them! And you, son of an annoying Iberian chieftain, are freed from bondage.'

He turned and gestured to Livia. 'You, too, are freed.' His eyes fell on Felix. 'And you – what is your wish?'

'M-me?' Felix stammered. 'Oh, nothing. I'm just happy to be home. Looking forward to my mother's cooking ...'

'Does she have cake?' the chicken demanded.

'Well, she—'

'That's it,' declared Caesar. He sounded happy now. Addressing the crowd once more he said, 'To this young man I grant the gift of a sacred chicken of Rome.' Scooping up the chicken, he thrust it at Felix. 'There. It's yours. And remind me to give you that dratted carpet before you leave. It's almost as annoying as the bird.'

'Er, thanks.' Felix stood there, clutching the chicken, who was muttering to itself.

'What am I, a parcel? Hand me here, hand me there. No, I am not a parcel. I am a *sacred chicken*.'

Titus appeared at Felix's side, distracting him from the chicken's complaints. 'What are your plans now, Felix? Will you go back to the army?'

Felix shuddered. 'Oh no. No way.'

'Don't tremble like that,' said the chicken. 'It makes me nauseous.'

The poet smiled. 'Good, because I have a proposition for you. If it hadn't been for you, I never would have thought to rhyme *Caesar* with *Alesia*. And your recount of your journey from Belgica to my island inspired me to write again. You have the heart of a poet and the soul of a storyteller. Come and work as my apprentice. I shall be your mentor.'

'I – wow,' said Felix. 'I'd love to. Thank you.'

'We can continue work on the epic of your journey.' He looked at the sacred chicken in Felix's arms. 'You know, I still haven't found a good rhyme for chicken …'

Felix thought for a moment. 'Thicken? Sicken?'

Livia joined them. 'Sicken sounds about right,' she said, but there was no heat in her words. In fact, she was beaming. 'Isn't it wonderful how everything has worked out? I'm sorry you got lumped with the chicken, though.'

'I'm not,' said Felix. 'Think about it, Livia – all this good fortune is thanks to the sacred chicken. The chicken gave me Vercingetorix's ring, and it was with General Cluvius when he gave King Juba's sceptre to the captain of the *Tarshish*. We were remembering the sacred chicken when I saw those thieves take Cleopatra's coins in Alexandria. And I only stopped at the carpet shop in Tadmor and found the magic carpet because of the golden chicken on the sign. So, you see, we owe the sacred chicken everything.' He gave the chicken a squeeze.

'No hugging!' The chicken struggled in Felix's embrace.

'You're right,' said Livia. 'Here, let me give it a hug too.'

'I said no hugging!'

Felix put the chicken down and it began to straighten its feathers indignantly.

Titus gazed at the chicken absently, whispering to himself. *'Too much cake and its waist will thicken?* No, not evocative enough.'

At the front of the box, Caesar was polishing the Gaulish chieftain's ring against his toga, one foot on the rolled-up carpet, trying to take the sceptre from the child, while jingling the box of coins. He was clearly very pleased, but something about the scene troubled Felix. He tried to put it into words.

'All these treasures we gave to Caesar don't just symbolise the conquest of other countries – it's the conquest of other *people*. When I was in the army I used to dream of being part of a great victory. Now I'm glad I never was. Those battles are all about winning power and wealth, but what do you do with them once you've got them?'

'I know what you mean,' said Livia. 'Power and wealth only matter if you're going to do something good with them. People matter more. *Freedom* matters more.' She smiled as she saw her brother enter the box. 'We're free! Maybe Marcus and I can even return to our parents' homeland in Iberia.' She frowned. 'Wherever that is.'

'Oh yes, that's an excellent plan,' said Titus, breaking off his muttering. 'But first, why don't you and your brother stay with me for a while? Felix and I can research your family history and find out more about your parents and how they came to be in Rome. Why, I'll bet it's an epic tale. And if you and your brother return to your homeland, it will have a happy ending!'

Felix agreed it was a good plan, though he didn't feel quite so pleased about the thought of Livia leaving Rome.

Then Titus turned to him. 'What do you think, Felix? Perhaps one day you might even travel to Iberia to write the epic of Livia and her brother.'

'Oh yes!' said Livia, clapping her hands.

'Go to Iberia? But he's only just arrived back in Rome!' said a voice behind Felix.

He spun around. 'Mum!'

'I thought you were in Belgica with General Porcius,' said his mother.

'I'm finished with the army,' Felix told her. 'I'm going to be a poet.'

'I hope the rations are better,' said his mother. 'Look at you! You're all skin and bones. The army can't have been feeding you very well. Now that you're back in Rome I'm going to have to feed you up. I'll start by baking a big cake. Lots of big cakes!'

'Yes please,' said Felix.

Squawk!

'Ahem,' said the chicken.

'Oh, right,' said Felix. 'Er, Mum, is it okay if I bring this sacred chicken?'

For once, the sacred chicken appeared to be satisfied. 'I like you!' it said to Felix's mother approvingly. 'Let's go home.'

The Chicken's Curse

An epic poem by Titus Magius

A serpent of enormous size,
A flash of lightning breaks the skies;
Ill omens for the army of Rome—
Our hero decides to flee for home.

In the dark forest a squawk is heard
A noble girl or a sacred bird?
Both girl and chicken are on the run
And now our heroes are three, not one

The road to Rome they must quickly find
For the general's men are close behind.
Felix's future is looking grim
As his pursuers catch up with him …

The pursuers are not who we thought
But one of three friends still will be caught
A scene ensues with terror and fear;
The way ahead has become less clear.

The plot has unexpectedly turned;
A secret once hidden now is learned.
But friends will never be forsaken—
A daring rescue's undertaken.

Evading capture our heroes change course
Heading west on the back of a horse
Yet the forest conceals prying eyes
And dawn reveals a nasty surprise.

So on foot to Lutetia they go,
Livia quick and the chicken slow.
With cake on offer the chicken leaves
(It's a loss that only Felix grieves.)

Another secret is brought to light
Explaining Livia's urgent flight:
They must reach Rome before it's too late
To save her brother from a dire fate.

Their passage by ship to Rome is sought
And found in Gaul's busy southern port.
That night, aboard a Phoenician barque,
Felix spies a strange scene in the dark.

A sailor recklessly clips his nails;
The ship is forced to lower her sails,
The mast is broken, waves pound the deck—
Who will survive a tragic shipwreck?

On an isle of banishment we find
A story's power to move a mind,
But the way to leave the island's shore
Sends our heroes far off course once more.

In the land of crocodile and kite
Lurk shady fellows, thieves in the night.
Felix gives chase, though risking his life
To a dark alley and the blade of a knife.

Foreign tales and a hungry bird
Foil the perilous plan overheard.
However, their action finds our pair
In possession of a treasure rare.

The loss of golden coins detected,
Our heroes are falsely suspected.
But the pair gives the soldiers the slip
Over sand on a new kind of ship.

Time unspools across the desert sand …
How to reach Rome from this distant land?
As a plot is hatched our heroes learn
There is yet graver cause for concern.

An oasis, but no shelter here
From those who trade in treason and fear.
Then, at the moment of greatest need,
An omen leads to magical speed.

Weary travellers sight home at last
But, oh, the disappointment is vast
To complete a journey, long and hard
And find the gates of the city barred.

His final triumph brings Caesar near;
Livia seeks to attract his ear.
On this a happy outcome depends,
But old foes are waiting for our friends.

In the arena, hearts full of dread;
So this is where their adventure led:
A sacrifice to Roman glory …
Or another end to the story?

With great rejoicing this epic ends
Freedom is granted to all our friends.
And if the listener rejoices too,
For your kindness, the poet thanks you.

Author's Note

You might have guessed that some details of *The Chicken's Curse* are made up – the talking camel, say, or the grumpy magic carpet – but it might surprise you to know what I didn't make up: the sacred chickens! Ancient Romans were very superstitious, and they really did consult sacred chickens on the eve of a battle (and Publius Claudius Pulcher really was so reckless as to disregard them). In fact, all the omens and superstitions mentioned (even the belief that clipping your nails aboard a ship is bad luck), as well as the legends and stories – from the sacred geese of Rome to the legend of Osiris and Isis – can be found in historical sources. The grand finale also has a basis in fact: in April 46 BC Julius Caesar celebrated a quadruple triumph. The song in which he's called 'smelly old Cheeser', though? Definitely made up!

Acknowledgements

When a sacred chicken insists that you transcribe its epic tale, if you want good fortune you have no choice but to obey. And because I heeded the chicken's demands, good fortune was mine: my journey was favoured with the wise counsel of David Francis, the publishing flair of Anna McFarlane, the keen editorial skill of Nicola Santilli, the eagle eyes of proofreader Vanessa Lanaway, the formidable illustrative talent of Kelly Canby, the creative design of Mika Tabata and the sage advice of Jane Novak. Thank you, and thanks to everyone at Allen & Unwin.

About the Author

Frances Watts is the author of more than 25 books for children, including the bestselling picture book *Kisses for Daddy* (illustrated by David Legge), which has been published in 20 languages; *Parsley Rabbit's Book about Books* (illustrated by David Legge), a Children's Book Council of Australia Book of the Year; and *Goodnight, Mice!* (illustrated by Judy Watson), winner of the Prime Minister's Literary Award for Children's Fiction. She is also the author of the medieval Sword Girl series (illustrated by Gregory Rogers) as well as two young adult novels, *The Raven's Wing* and *The Peony Lantern*. Frances lives in Sydney, Australia.